MEDLEY OF MURDER

MEDLEY OF MURDER

Compiled and Edited by

Susan Budavari and Suzanne Flaig

Red Coyote Press, LLC
Phoenix, Arizona
www.redcoyotepress.com

Copyright Acknowledgments

"The Library Murders," Copyright © 2005 by CR Bolinski
"In Memory of Maggie," Copyright © 2005 by Susan Budavari
"The Last Habano," Copyright © 2005 by Howard B. Carron
"Ephemera," Copyright © 2005 by Suzanne Flaig
"Identity Theft," Copyright © 2005 by Patricia Klemme
"Stella," Copyright © 2005 by Deborah J Ledford
"Call From Beyond," Copyright © 2005 by Reva Spiro Luxenberg
"Smalltown Heart," Copyright © 2005 by Barbara McArthur
"Fast Pace," Copyright © 2005 by Robin Merrill
"A Gift For Details," Copyright © 2005 by Alan M. Petrillo
"His Little Darling," Copyright © 2005 by Maralee Reiner
"Incident on Main Street," Copyright © 2005 by Michèle Stapley
"Bohemian Rhapsody," Copyright © 2005 by Maria Grazia Swan
"Murder in Mind," Copyright © 2005 by Audrey Thibodeau
"Eye Strain," Copyright © 2005 by Sybil Yeaman and Rachelle Yeaman

This is a work of fiction. All the characters, places, and events portrayed in these short stories are either fictitious or are used fictitiously.

Lyrics Acknowledgment
Bohemian Rhapsody
Words and Music by Freddie Mercury
© 1975 (Renewed 2003) B. FELDMAN & CO., LTD., Trading as TRIDENT MUSIC
All Rights Controlled and Administered by GLENWOOD MUSIC CORP.
All Rights Reserved International Copyright Secured Used by permission

Cover photograph Copyright © 2005 by Susan Budavari

ISBN 0-9766733-6-3
Library of Congress Control Number: 2005907419

Red Coyote Press, LLC
Phoenix, Arizona 85082
www.redcoyotepress.com

CONTENTS

INTRODUCTION

Welcome to this anthology of fifteen distinctly different tales of mystery and suspense. They present a taste of the various popular sub-genres, including cozy, hard-boiled, police procedural, romantic suspense, historical, and psychological drama. Some have touches of humor, irony and even the supernatural. Like a medley of musical pieces, these diverse stories are linked together by the common theme: murder.

The contributing authors came to Arizona from states across America and have drawn upon varied perspectives and individual experiences for their stories. Here, amid the beautiful natural surroundings and nourished by the support of their fellow authors and by members of the local publishing community, all have pursued their craft.

We hope this volume provides you with pleasurable moments and provokes thought. We also hope that you enjoy this anthology as much as we've enjoyed creating it. If you wish to contact us, please go to www.redcoyotepress.com.

A special note of thanks to Donna Hanna who provided insightful comments and pointers on punctuation and grammar.

Susan Budavari and Suzanne Flaig
Phoenix, Arizona

SMALLTOWN HEART

Barbara McArthur

Gladys Phelps Rogers sat on the top rail of the bridge dangling her bare feet. The high water of the Verde River raged and boiled with the fury of a hundred wild mustangs, taking chunks of the riverbank with it as it thundered beneath her. Last night's storms upstate had caused this violent run-off. There would be no ducks looking to be fed today.

As the water hit a rocky obstacle, spray rose high in the air, drenching Gladys from head to foot. She pushed several strands of straight, long gray-brown hair back off her forehead, and wiped tears from her red-rimmed, swollen gray eyes. All traces of her carefully-applied makeup were gone. Her pink organdy party dress with rosettes across the bodice clung to her slender, boyish body and felt cold against her skin.

With two fingers, she peeled the envelope from her pocket and waved it in the air in a futile attempt to dry it. It was soaked—her name now only a faint blur on its surface. Suddenly, a gust of wind caught it and carried it away. She watched as the envelope sailed up briefly, then fell into the water, where it quickly disappeared.

What difference did it make? Without reading the note inside, she knew what it said. She had read the sad words many times before. Sending a note was always easier than delivering bad news in person. There was no return address and no postmark. She would never know where he was now. It was plain to her that he did not mean to come back.

Gladys's thoughts returned to the party. Four days of rain had given way to the most beautiful, blue skies with just a few wispy clouds. The house and gardens had never looked more festive. Bowls of spring flowers adorned pink-skirted tables on the porch. Her mother's fine china set a regal tone, and the buffet table was laden with delicacies she had been preparing for days. Everything was perfect. Gladys smiled as she thought how pleased her mother would have been with all of her efforts.

She had checked her appearance in the hall mirror every time she walked by. The upswept hair would be a surprise to everyone, and so would the makeup. She liked the way the beige foundation cleared her skin and gave it a rosier glow. It had been worth the hours she spent getting it just right.

Everyone came. Most of the townspeople, many of whom she had worked with at the mill, came. Hardly able to contain their excitement and curiosity, they wanted to meet the wonderful man who would finally remove Gladys from Woodenville's list of unmarriageable spinsters.

She heard them whispering to each other as they always did.

"Gladys, of course, is not a pretty girl, but she's such a nice girl."

"All that money and property but so unlucky in love."

"She was married once, you know, for less than a year. Nobody knows what actually happened, but we were all sure he was only interested in her money."

"Since then, how many have there been? Three lovely young men who all backed off as soon as marriage was discussed. Her attorney probably wanted them to sign an agreement."

"Something must be wrong. Something drives them away."

"Soiled goods," one said mysteriously, but when pressed, couldn't or wouldn't say why.

"Just shows that even money can't buy love," they concluded.

But maybe this time it had.

"Don't listen to them, Gladys," her mother would have said. *"They mean well and they truly love and want the best for you. They're just harmless old busy-bodies who have always had too much to say about us. Just smile and ignore them!"*

"It's a beautiful party, Gladys…your mother would be so proud of you. I can't wait to meet your young man." Myrna Holbrook had been her father's secretary and her mother's best friend at one time—until the mill closed and Myrna lost her job. Myrna changed. Something fell apart that never quite mended.

Despite the hint of insincerity in Myrna's voice, Gladys gave her a hug.

The guests sipped their wine and waited to meet this wondrous man whom no one had seen, only heard about—this fabled man, a writer, who loved Gladys, and, "very reluctantly" accepted Gladys's check for $50,000 to publish his book. Oh yes, they had that on very good authority directly from Tom Barwood, the banker.

When the letter came by courier, every guest stopped talking and turned to fasten inquiring eyes on the envelope carried relentlessly, mercilessly toward Gladys. Across the wide, green expanse of lawn it came. Gladys knew its contents.

"I am not coming back. I never loved you. I only wanted your money. You stupid girl, how could anyone like me ever love someone like you?"

He would not say these things in so many words, of course. David was a talented writer and had a gift for saying difficult things very diplomatically.

She opened the letter. Where were her glasses? Without her glasses, she couldn't see a thing. It didn't matter. She knew the words by heart.

She composed herself. Something she did very well.

Her mask in place, she smiled widely and exclaimed a little too brightly, "Oh, no…what a pity! David's been held up and won't be here today after all. His publisher simply insists that he stay over to approve some revisions!"

The guests murmured their disappointment. They hugged her and reassured her and wished her well. As they ate her food, drank her wine and said all the appropriate things, they whispered knowingly to each other. They had expected as much, they said. It was all too good to be true, they said. Here we go, again, they said. Poor Gladys, poor Gladys.

When at last, all the guests had left, Gladys walked down to the river, along the path where she and David had walked hand in hand. She sat on the rail where they sat. Gladys thought about what had happened …again.

She looked down into the whirlpool swirling beneath her feet. It looked frightening and cold. Then she saw something beautiful. The muddy, brown waters of the river became green at the edges of the whirlpool, and where the waters tightened into a perfect circle, the green darkened and deepened until the center, the part that led to that inviting nothingness, was the color of emeralds. Emeralds that sparkled with snow-white foam.

She could feel the icy pinpricks of spray on her arms, not unlike the goose bumps she felt the first time David touched her. Then she sensed the hand at her lower back, just as David's hand often slid to that sensuous curve.

She heard a familiar voice saying, "It's better this way, Gladys…it's so much better this way."

As she turned her head, she felt the push, she fell against the bridge rail, and slid flailing and screaming into the waters below.

A pink rosette lay lodged in the grasses at river's edge.

Deputy Smith found it and handed it to the sheriff.

"Did you know her, sir?"

"I knew her whole family, son. Made their money in logging. You should have seen those trucks loaded with timber coming down from the White Mountains before the environmentalists shut them down."

"I heard they were logging out the forests, sir. I heard…"

Sheriff Crowley ignored the younger man.

"Gladys, when she was young, I called her Gladdy… grew up in Woodenville. It wasn't always easy for her. When the Phelps Mill shut down about twelve years ago, a lot of jobs were lost, and there was resentment. Not the Phelpses' fault, but some people just couldn't see it. So there they were, living in that big old white house up on the hill. Folks were pretty sore at the family. No matter what Phelps tried to do for the town, it wasn't enough. After college, Gladdy pretty much kept to herself. Buried herself in the accounting office at the mill until it closed."

"I heard . . ." the deputy tried to interject.

"Listen and learn, son. Wasn't long after . . . she lost her parents. I couldn't tell you what she did after that, except she put on an "Easter Egg Roll" and a "Visit With Santa" for the kids every year. Her parents always had something for the kids, even after the mill closed, and Gladys kept the tradition going."

"I remember last year's Christmas party. Ms. Rogers was nice . . . not very pretty . . . but really nice . . .," Deputy Smith offered.

"In some ways, I blame her mother for this. Shielded Gladys from all the trouble. Never taught her to see what was real and face trouble head on. Mrs. Phelps always had a smile for everyone. Just sailed through as though everything was always wonderful. Sometimes I wondered if she could see the way things were at all. Maybe there was a problem there...mentally, you know. Mr. Phelps just kept doing for the town, Mrs. Phelps kept smiling...and the town kept resenting," he said, as they walked back across the bridge to the police car.

"Then, there's no doubt this is an accident, sir...a suicide?" Deputy Smith had only been on the force six months.

"No doubt, son. If you'd been around here as long as I have, you'd understand how well I know these people. This poor girl had problems that would have made anybody jump into the river. It's all over town. Her latest boyfriend pulled a disappearing act. She'd had enough."

"But . . ." Deputy Smith remembered his training.

"No 'buts,' son . . . this was a plain and simple suicide. You can take that to the bank." The sheriff had that "edge" in his voice that said, *"that's enough . . . that's the way it's going to be."*

Tom Crowley had been sheriff of Woodenville for thirty years, and he hated it when one of his own jumped into the river. He looked at the swift current and, checking his watch, timed a piece of wood as it traveled downstream.

"Son, call the Green Valley substation. Tell them to watch for the body."

Sheriff Crowley knew Gladys would wash up on the sandbar down river sometime around ten that night.

Hannah Royce, owner of "Styles by Hannah" was holding court. The aroma of permanent solution and nail polish solvent hung heavily in the air causing eyes to water.

"She never came in here once. Always cut her own hair. It showed."

Hannah's latex-gloved fingers dripped red as she applied henna to Joy Feldon's thinning gray hair.

"*Great Expectations* just waiting to happen, I say," said Ruth Newberry, the librarian. "Decaying old wedding dress, all that dust and cobwebs. She could have sat up in that big old house of hers for years."

"Much better, yes, she's much better off. How much bad luck can one person take?" said Mary Littleton, the manicurist. "Did you see her nails at that party? It's obvious she was doing all her own gardening."

They felt they had to attend. There was no family left to mourn Gladys. No one to call. Her mother and father had been killed nearly ten years before in a fiery head-on collision with the town's largest cottonwood tree. Some townsfolk remembered the event in such detail that faces grew pale and heads turned away just hearing the story retold.

They had done their duty back then. They brought casseroles and cakes and sent flowers. Some had been able to put the past behind them and show genuine sorrow at Gladys's loss. Others thought the Phelps got what was coming to them.

And so it was that over three hundred people who knew Gladys in the last thirty-eight years crowded into Paterson's Funeral Home to hear Pastor Martin of the Woodenville Community Church praise Gladys's philanthropy.

"We'll be forever grateful for our beautiful library," he intoned, "and the magnificent collection of books that her contribution provided."

There was a rustle of folks whispering and turning inquisitively to their neighbors, as very few knew that Gladys had anything to do with the library.

"And the diagnostic technology in the children's wing of the clinic," he went on. "And the playground equipment in Verde River Park." Inquiring looks and shoulder shrugging rippled through the congregation in a wave.

"And the Jaycees college scholarship fund that allows two deserving local students to enroll at the state university for a four year course of study. This program has been funded entirely by Gladys Phelps Rogers for the last ten years. I am pleased to say that, due to Gladys's foresight and concern for the young people of our community, this program will continue as long as there is a town of Woodenville."

A crescendo of "I didn't know that, did you?" and "I thought all those spaghetti dinners..." was being voiced aloud at this point.

"Perhaps we should remember, too, the parties Gladys gave for the children, which all of you enjoyed. Gladys continued the Phelps' holiday traditions long after the mill closed. Has any town ever had such splendid celebrations of Easter and Christmas?

"Although Gladys did not want recognition for any of her gifts, I feel it would be entirely appropriate if a plaque bearing her name were affixed to the monument in the town square, beside the names of Woodenville's other benefactors."

Heads were nodding "yes." There was a murmur of guilty approval.

"Surely the gates of Heaven will open wide to accept such an angel," Pastor Martin went on. "And surely this angel will find the happiness in Heaven that escaped her on this earth."

The pallbearers stepped forward, signaling the beginning of the procession to Green Acres Cemetery next to the funeral home. The pallbearers had been chosen by Doc Wellborn, Gladys's doctor from the day she was born. Rod Schafer, the town's only attorney, Todd Brown and Jeff Pierce, two recent recipients of college scholarships, Peter Redfield, the town pharmacist, Charlie Knight, custodian of the library and Tom Crowley, the sheriff, hoisted the flower-laden casket onto their shoulders.

The white casket with brass handles was covered with pink carnations. The flowers had been chosen by the ladies of the church. No one really knew Gladys well enough to know which flowers had been her favorites, but everyone agreed that pink carnations were always a safe choice.

Outside, a soft rain was falling, and followers opened their umbrellas as they left the funeral home. Sam Potts, the funeral director, stood at the door handing large black umbrellas to those who had forgotten to bring one. Some made a quick decision to forego the graveside service and sprinted toward their cars. The loyal pulled their coats about them and bent into the rain, following the casket.

The burial site was canopied and the rows of dry chairs were filling up quickly.

"Such a shame," Adelaide Schafer was saying to no one in particular and anyone who would listen.

"But didn't you really expect this to happen eventually?" whispered Joan Redfield, her eyes peeking out from a wet silk scarf wound around her head.

Myrna Holbrook's short gray hair was plastered to her head, and she mopped her face with a make-up-stained handkerchief.

"Just like her parents. Maybe it was just her time," Myrna sniffed. She set her lips in a firm line. "It was her time." As if that settled it.

"Yes, but look at all she had to give and all she gave, and we never knew it. Never had a chance to thank her for any of it." This voice belonged to Nancy Becker, the mayor's wife, who rarely voiced an opinion on anything.

"Gladys never had a real friend in this town, and we should all be ashamed," said Doc Wellborn, ending the conversation.

When he bowed his head, rainwater that had collected in the brim of his old tan fedora emptied on the seat in front of him.

Pastor Martin was reading a passage from the Bible, his words garbled by the now steady downpour and a wind that had suddenly come up. The green canvas canopy flaps whipped and snapped, and the roof sagged low with the weight of the rain.

The service was finally over and everyone stood, moving back and forth slowly, no one wanting to be the first to leave. As they gained the courage to disperse, they saw, some distance away, a tall man in a black raincoat standing against the trunk of a large cottonwood tree. The sodden branches of the tree hung low around him like a shroud.

His wide, black western hat was pulled down to meet wraparound dark glasses, almost hiding his face completely. He held a bouquet of white tulips. He raised one hand, which brought a man to his side.

Ignoring the crowd, which had stopped open-mouthed to watch, the two men, arm in arm, slowly approached the gravesite. The tall man walked with some uncertainty, appearing to need support.

Finally, he stood beside the casket. He reached out and touched it, and found a place for the tulips at the center of the carnation blanket. Putting both hands on the casket, he leaned against it and bowed his head.

The assembly was stunned and silent. All eyes were riveted on his back, which moved almost imperceptibly, but surely, as though he were crying.

Suddenly, the man turned, and finding his companion's ready arm, began to move away. His stumbling gait betrayed, beyond any doubt, his desperate, raw grief.

He was quickly lost in the shadows of a rapidly descending darkness.

The mourners moved along…some, crying noisily, unable to mask their sudden feelings of grief . . . and others, in silence.

The downpour continued relentlessly.

Only Tom Crowley and Myrna Holbrook remained. They sat under the canopy beside the casket.

"Who was that man, Sheriff? Oh, God, do you suppose that was her writer?"

"I don't know, Mrs. Holbrook. Maybe this will tell us."

He reached in his inside pocket and brought out the letter that had been found on the sandbar near Gladys's body.

It was dry now. If it had been written in ink, the message would surely have disappeared, but, because it had been written on a typewriter especially designed for the blind, the message was crystal clear:

"Darling,

How I miss you. I have the best news. Baxter will publish my book without a subsidy! Can you imagine, darling . . . they love my book and will pay me an advance!

They want me to stay over to sign contracts. All our dreams will come true now, and I owe everything to the only one in the world who believed in me . . . you, darling! I'll miss the party that meant so much to you, but I'll see you on Friday. I love you, Gladdy.
David"

Mrs. Holbrook doubled over, moaning as if in pain.

Sheriff Crowley didn't know what to do, so he patted her back and hoped she would pull herself together. He'd had enough drama for one day. He walked away, leaving Mrs. Holbrook to grieve.

He wanted to get to the office to make some copies. Crow would be served in every home in Woodenville tonight.

Deputy Smith was sitting quietly at his desk, deep in thought, when the sheriff returned. He had just gone through Gladys's clothing, boxed, tagged and filed it. Nothing of value that anybody would want. But his mind was still on the clump of dry dough he had found in one of the pockets of her pink party dress. *If she brought bread to feed the ducks, was she planning to kill herself?* He guessed when he'd been in

Woodenville as long as Sheriff Crowley, he'd be able to figure things like this out.

"Beautiful service except for the rain…and you really missed the excitement. Gladys's lover boy showed up with flowers. Blind, he is. That explains a lot." He reached in his pocket.

"Take a look at this note. Looks like Gladys jumped the gun. Make me ten copies." Sheriff Crowley took off his hat and shook it before making a perfect toss to the hat rack.

Deputy Smith read the note the sheriff handed him, and moved to the copy machine. This was getting too complicated. Way over his head. He had planned to say something about the dough, but now . . . well, Sheriff Crowley really had this one all buttoned up. Deputy Smith decided it wasn't worth his job to get him all riled up again.

A year later, Baxter Publishing announced the publication of a new book. The debut novel, receiving raves, was to be introduced in Woodenville, which had been the inspiration for its title and theme, "*Smalltown Heart.*" The author, David Todd, was blind, but had been able to describe the town and its people with such clarity that it was hard to believe he had never seen any of them or the town for himself. His depiction of life and love in a small town was destined to put Woodenville on the map.

It was with some trepidation that the townspeople lined up to receive the first copies available. Some began to read before leaving the store. People were reading as they walked back to their cars.

Ruth Newberry, the librarian, who had taken a speed reading course, was the first to finish. She wiped away her tears and added the damp tissue to those in her pocket. Grabbing her coat, she drove to "Styles by Hannah."

"She saw only beauty," she said to Hannah, Joy, and Adelaide, assembled there for the weekly ritual.

Mary Littleton put down her emery board.

"Gladys saw the town as perfect, and all of us as warm, caring, loving people. She passed this on to David Todd, and he has preserved us all as Gladys saw us. I've never been more ashamed in my life. All that poor girl ever wanted was love, and we . . ., because we were so stupid . . ., we were so sure . . ."

"What are you talking about, Ruth? Gladys was a lovely girl, so generous and warm. Everyone loved her!" said Joy, her fiery red hair in tight wet ringlets all over her head.

"And she gave wonderful parties," added Adelaide, "and she made all the food herself."

"Do you remember her garden?" asked Mary. "Absolutely beautiful, and she tended each and every plant and flower so lovingly. Her home should have been in *House and Garden!*"

"And her hair . . . so naturally beautiful! Gladys was one of those lucky ones. Why, if everyone had hair like Gladys's, I'd be out of business!" proclaimed Hannah.

David Todd never returned to Woodenville.

Myrna Holbrook, confined at the Woodenville Institute for the Insane, has not spoken a word since she was found at Gladys Phelps Rogers's gravesite, attempting to throw herself into the grave during the interment.

Myrna had never been "quite right," they all agreed.

INCIDENT ON MAIN STREET

Michèle Stapley

Useless ribbons of shade slipped from the row of palm trees along Scottsdale's Main Street, limped across the burning sidewalk and squiggled over whatever sculpture stood in the way, temporarily amputating the limb of a child, a pig, or an Indian scout. The nature of the amputation was not accidental, but rather the inevitable result of a variety of circumstances—the shape of the sculpture, the distance from the palm tree, the time of day, the day of the year, how sunny or overcast the sky. But few gallery owners on Main Street, whose business it was to sell the sculptures, ever noticed the amputations or wondered how they came to be.

This afternoon, if they chanced to look out their windows at all, they would simply notice the street was quiet. This would not disappoint them, however, since they were busy preparing for the evening's ArtWalk, the first of the season. The more experienced among them understood a successful opening was not accidental, but rather the inevitable result of a variety of circumstances. Although unable to guarantee clear skies or a bull market, they made every effort to procure the other essentials—salable art, a reliable caterer and a few well-heeled collectors.

To this end, Joyce Evans had secured new work by painter Ardeth Nelson, made arrangements with Ruby, the most reliable caterer in town, and sent personal invitations to wealthy collectors such as Toni Gates, who had expressed an interest in Ardeth's new paintings. Confident these ladies would fill the role assigned to them for the evening—painter, caterer, collector—Joyce relaxed. It was three o'clock.

At three-thirty, Ardeth Nelson parked near a bronze toddler, pulled twenty paintings from her van and hauled them, two at a time, across the hot sidewalk into the cool of the Joyce Evans Gallery. She propped the paintings along the three walls reserved for her show and waited, nervous and perspiring, for Joyce's reaction.

Joyce took her sweet time, walking slowly from one painting to the next, fist at her chin, index finger jabbing her cheek, high heels clicking on the hard wood floor. When she reached the end of the third wall, she turned and headed back, click, click.

"Rather nice," she finally said, then added, "The color harmonies are a little tired, though, don't you think?" She stopped in front of the smallest painting—two nuns in long black habits walking past a row of brightly colored Vespas—and bent forward slightly. "Actually, this one works very well."

Ardeth winced. *Actually, this one works very well?* That's it? A year of hard work, a small fortune in custom frames, an expensive trip to Italy, and that's it? Oh, and *the color harmonies are a little tired.* Shit.

Ardeth pushed her hands deep into her jean pockets, hunched her shoulders and mumbled into her t-shirt, "I don't see what's wrong with the color harmonies. I think the color works very well. Besides, I sent you photographs of the paintings and you never complained about the color."

"Photographs lie, you know that. And yes, the color does work well. But it's all so obvious, don't you see? And the obvious is always a little vulgar."

Vulgar? She thinks the color is *vulgar?* The paintings aren't about color. They aren't even about Italy. They're about irony: the modern juxtaposed with the ancient, the secular with the religious, the poverty with the splendor. Can't she see that?

"But the irony is good, Ardeth. I do like the irony."

Ardeth bit her lip and glanced over at her favorite painting. In it, a young woman in a revealing sundress is standing in the sumptuous Pitti Palace in Florence, glancing over her shoulder at a painting of St. Agnes, the chaste fourth century martyr. Ardeth hoped Joyce would hang that one alone on the freestanding wall facing the front window. Spotlighted from above, it would attract attention with its gold and scarlet accents and the provocative stance of the young woman in the sundress. But she made no such recommendation.

"Let's spread these out," Joyce said to her assistant, a tall girl with spiked red hair and black eyeliner. "Move these two over there and bring the vertical back here...yes, that's good..."

With one hand fisted on her narrow hip, the other flashing a perfectly manicured index finger at one painting after another, Joyce planted herself in the center of her gallery, issuing instructions in a clipped monotone. She was dressed in a gray silk pantsuit, her silver hair in a meticulous pageboy.

Ardeth sat cross-legged on the floor, waiting to see where the large painting would be hung. First, it was moved to the center of the long wall where it overpowered the paintings on either side. Later, it was put along the wall farthest from the window, immediately losing its impact.

Finally, after an hour of rearranging, it was placed against the freestanding wall, exactly where Ardeth had wanted it all along.

Once the paintings were arranged in their assigned order on the floor, the harried assistant finished the job, nailing them to the freshly painted walls so they were precisely spaced and, regardless of size or shape, at eye level for the viewer of average eight. A perfect gallery mount.

"For heaven's sake, Ardeth, get up off the floor," Joyce said, as she picked up a stack of brochures and handed one to Ardeth. "They're very handsome, don't you think? I didn't include the biographical notes you gave me; that would have ruined the design. I prefer simplicity, as you know."

She certainly did, thought Ardeth, scanning the gallery with its white walls and polished wood floor and paintings hung so far apart that one seemed totally unrelated to the next. And now the brochures. Four of her paintings were beautifully reproduced on heavy white paper, but not even the titles had been permitted to clutter the handsome design. Instead, they were listed in tiny print on the back.

"Don't you think people want to know about the artist? And see the titles with the paintings?" asked Ardeth, aware that a slight whine had crept into her voice.

"Art speaks for itself or not at all," Joyce pronounced, removing the few objects from her glass desktop to allow room for the brochures that she fanned out in a perfect arc. "And you, my dear, are presenting art, not clever titles."

"But when Shannon Gallagher's paintings were published in *Western Art Review*, there was a long article about how well the titles defined her work. And you know how popular she became..."

"Is that what you want, Ardeth? To be popular? Would you prefer being popular to being excellent?" Joyce waved her finger in Ardeth's face. "You're still very young, simply not ready for that kind of exposure. And you should know by now that I will never, ever give permission for any painting hanging in this gallery to be reproduced in *Western Art Review*."

Ardeth flushed at the reprimand and felt a familiar rebellion, the kind she associated with sixth grade, when Sister Mary Irene humiliated her in front of the entire class for admitting she wanted to be famous. Well, what was wrong with that, wanting to be famous like Georgia O'Keefe?

"You will be changing your clothes, of course," Joyce declared.

Ardeth looked down at her jeans and Birkenstocks. "Yeah, I brought my basic black, just like I promised."

"Good. You can use the powder room to change. And for heaven's sake, pick up your backpack and get it out of sight." Joyce fluttered her hand at the offending object.

Ardeth gathered her things, marched to the powder room and hissed "bitch" under her breath. She hung the hated black dress on a hook and threw her black pumps in the corner. Frowning at the very thought of wearing them, she caught sight of the frown in the vanity mirror. Her reflection alarmed her. It distressed her to see she was homelier than she hoped, square and sullen-faced. She released the frown with an effort. Make-up would help, she told her reflection. It always did.

Then she recalled the plan she had put in place this morning. Delight spread across her face, softening the lines, tilting the head, flushing her cheeks. She would get decked out, not for Joyce, not even for the ArtWalk crowd, always chic and usually a tad drunk, but for the reporter and cameraman from Channel 10 News who had accepted her invitation to the opening. She had convinced the station that a lively art reception in a gallery on Main Street would make a nice addition to the evening news, especially on a Thursday night when not much else was happening.

Naturally, she had not told Joyce, who would surely view this as far more vulgar than appearing in *Western Art Review*. But at least tonight thousands of people would see her paintings—thousands—even if it was on TV. If all went well, she would be a little bit famous, and that was something.

At five o'clock, Ruby walked into her bedroom, opened her dresser drawer and smiled down at the red lace push-up bra and matching thong she had purchased yesterday at Victoria's Secret. Selecting the lingerie was the one exciting thing she had done all week. If she had been looking for comfort, or even something that flattered her still slim but less than perfect body, she would have made another choice. But those were not her considerations.

Tonight, as she put on the thong and bra for the first time, Ruby felt like a new woman, daring, naughty, mysterious. Slipping into her black satin slacks, she was startled—no, delighted!—to feel the smooth fabric glide luxuriously over her bare butt. She swung her hips slowly, enjoying the caress of the garment, watching herself in the mirror. In a reverse strip tease, she added a tailored white shirt and a silk tie and then fluffed her auburn hair.

The shirt brushed gently against her nearly naked breasts, now artfully perched on tiny hammocks of red lace. She slid her hands down the front of her shirt to where she could feel the band of the thong under her slacks. Hesitating, she denied herself further pleasure and finished dressing. She slipped into a comfortable pair of crepe-soled loafers and returned to the kitchen.

Carefully removing several large, flat boxes from the refrigerator, she stacked them on the counter, checking each one off her list: one platter of fruit, another of cheese, two of tea sandwiches, one of stuffed mushrooms. The final box contained the smoked salmon canapés Joyce Evans always selected for her gallery openings.

"I'm off!" she shouted, hoping her mother would hear her so she wouldn't have to go into the den and poke her awake. At thirty-six years of age, Ruby was still required to report her comings and goings, although it was unclear why, since her mother rarely seemed to care. All she did was stare at the television all day. She even ate her meals in front of the set, not noticing whether Ruby brought her a sandwich and chips or something more elegant from the catering business. Her mother's sour, stale body odor permeated the den just as surely as her sour disposition had permeated everything else.

There was no response to Ruby's goodbye. She walked into the den and turned off the TV, just as effective a maneuver as poking her mother, while allowing Ruby to keep her distance. She needed to keep her distance, not just because of the odor, but because her mother's eyes were hollow and Ruby was afraid if she looked into them she might fall into the emptiness and disappear forever.

"Huh? What're you doing?" Her mother lifted her head off the recliner and frowned at the television. "Why'd you turn it off?"

"I'm leaving now, Mother. The job's at seven and I have a few things to pick up on the way."

"What time'll you be back?"

"Not late. Maybe ten."

"Ten? I'll be in bed by then. Now for heaven's sake turn the TV back on."

Ruby handed her the remote and walked out of the room. When she turned back to look, her mother was already staring at the television, pressing buttons until she found Channel 10.

Loading the cartons into the station wagon, Ruby wondered if it was possible to die of boredom. Afraid of being crushed by her mother's inertia, she continually searched for new ways to wiggle out from under it. And wiggle she did, desperate to avoid the panic attacks that had become so familiar that by now she knew exactly how long they would last—twenty minutes—and how they would end—with one exquisite moment of peace when the last drop of adrenaline had been released. Then her breathing would return to normal, leaving her limp, amazed she had survived the onslaught. She could never predict when the next panic attack would occur, or why, and she was unable to defend herself when one did.

She was too embarrassed to tell her counselor how much the attacks frightened her or the huge effort required to avoid them. A large part of that effort was devoted to treating herself to a new distraction each week. This week it was the red underwear. It could just as easily have been an exotic houseplant, or a new hairdo, or another trashy paperback, the kind where the heroine is flying a jet or exploring Nepal or sleeping with the police chief. But it was becoming more difficult each week, and she had finally reached the point where she was willing to die for some excitement, perhaps because she would surely die without it.

Dying was not warranted, her counselor assured her. Just move out of town, was her advice. Ruby said she would try, there was nothing she wanted more, in fact, than to move away. But she knew it would take a miracle or sheer brute force—certainly something beyond her own control—to get her out of town.

But even if she wouldn't be leaving town tonight, at least she was wearing her new red lingerie, and that was something.

At five-thirty, Toni Gates slipped into the passenger seat of a shiny gray Mercedes, inhaled the new-car smell rich with leather and slammed the door, pissed that Eddie had bought yet another car. He said it was for her, of course, for her fortieth birthday. Oh, sure. Then why the hell didn't he ask her what model she wanted, or what color, or something? Besides, he was spending too much money lately and that scared her almost as much as the fact that he was screwing someone else.

"Well, how do you like it?" Eddie asked, settling behind the wheel and adjusting the seat.

"Fine."

"*Fine?* Just *fine?* What's not to like?"

"What if I wanted white? Or blue? Why didn't you even ask me?"

"Ask you? Look, when a good deal comes along you take it and you don't ask to change the damn color." He turned on the ignition with a confident flip of the wrist. The engine responded with a seductive purr.

Toni adjusted her black lace shawl, exposing bare shoulders and a glimpse of her crimson dress. She had taken great care getting ready tonight because her husband's lover was several years younger and drop-dead gorgeous. But then, so was Eddie. He was also sexy, rich, and slightly dangerous. That was the intoxicating combination that mesmerized her when she became wife number three.

She met Eddie at a wedding five years ago. A business friend of the groom's, new in town, recently divorced and obviously flush with cash, he showed up in the wrong clothes, expensive but embarrassingly flashy, more suitable for Hollywood or Vegas. She, on the other hand, wore a borrowed designer dress, imitation pearls and stylish shoes purchased at an outlet store. As they danced cheek to cheek on the candlelit patio overlooking the golf course, he whispered in her ear that she was the classiest woman at the reception, and he needed someone to teach him class.

Anxious to assure him that his perceptions were accurate, she casually reminisced about her years at Harvard, never mentioning the grants that made her education possible. She embellished on her success in the corporate world, but naturally skipped the details of the price she paid to get ahead.

Eddie was an eager student. Once spruced up to her satisfaction, she led him to the altar, deliberately ignorant of the source of his income. She resigned from her job, devoted herself to shopping, decorating, entertaining and, of course, introducing Eddie to the right people.

The right people, it turned out, loved him. Even so, when left to his own devices, he gravitated to the tacky, the flamboyant, the slightly out-of-control world that lurked in the casinos outside of town. Money laundering, hit men, drugs. Revolting things. But the money, oh, she did love the money.

"Business must be good," Toni muttered. "Or did you have a good week at the tables?"

"Dammit, Toni, you know I never talk business. What the hell's the matter with you tonight?"

"Well, excuse me!" She flipped down the visor to check her reflection in the mirror. Too much make-up? Not enough? She patted her black hair where it was pulled back on one side, secured with a diamond barrette, last year's birthday present. She looked damn good for forty, she thought, except for the tension that flattened her mouth.

The tension had been there for days. Tension with a touch of panic. Had she done the smart thing when she mailed Gordon the photos of his wife and Eddie? She came across the pictures last week when they fell out of an old issue of *Sports Illustrated* she was carrying to the trash. After the initial shock, she studied the images so carefully she could even identify the hotel where their little romp had taken place.

Although she couldn't imagine Gordon's face when he opened the envelope and saw the evidence, she knew with certainty he would stop the affair quickly, and that's what mattered. He would rough up his faithless wife, humiliate her in front of her children, threaten to sell her horse, throw her out of the house, whatever it took. Men like Gordon, one of the casino regulars, knew how to control their wives but rarely confronted the men their wives became involved with, especially if they were wealthy and powerful, like Eddie. Of course, if a dispute more serious than an unfaithful wife arose, they could still avoid confrontation by hiring a hit man to exact revenge. Men were such cowards.

"Where is this restaurant, anyway?" Eddie asked.

"Right across from the Joyce Evans Gallery, on Main Street."

"Have we eaten there before?"

"No, it just opened. Got rave reviews."

"Any plans for after dinner?"

"The ArtWalk, I guess. Joyce sent us a personal invitation. She knows I want to see the new paintings by that young artist, the one who just returned from Italy."

"The ArtWalk's okay with me as long as we don't hang around too long," said Eddie. "I'm playing tennis tomorrow at six."

"Six? In the morning? Who the hell wants to play tennis that early?"

"Gordon. He called today. Haven't heard from him in a long time."

"Gordon called you? And wants to play tennis?"

"Yeah, why? You sound surprised. Anyway, I said fine, I'd love to."

Love to? How the hell can you talk so calmly about playing tennis with Gordon when you're screwing his wife, for god's sake? She wrapped her shawl tight around her shoulders.

Eddie added, "Gordon said he used to play a lot of tennis."

"Really?" That must have been before he gained all that weight, Toni mused. Under different circumstances, thoughts of Gordon's fleshy arms waving a tennis racquet would have amused her.

What in the world was Gordon up to? Perhaps she shouldn't have sent the photos. But what choice did she have? Her marriage was in trouble and it's not as if she had a lot of options. She certainly didn't have the leverage she used to have because now Eddie knew all the right people. He was, by every standard that really mattered, well connected, so if he decided to dump her tomorrow for a slut like Gordon's wife, nobody would even care. Right now her only choice was to shoot down the competition as soon as it appeared and try to think of a more permanent solution.

"Gordon wants to get back in shape," Eddie continued. "He says it'll give him an edge. Says it might even help in the bedroom, too. I told him he was damn right it would." His hand reached over to stroke Toni's thigh. "I told him it sure works for me."

Toni's right hand jumped to push his away, stopped midair, and patted her shawl instead. Then, in the soft, throaty voice she used when she wanted to distract him and regain her composure, she said, "You're right, Eddie. It sure does work for you." Reaching over, she placed her left hand on his thigh and squeezed it gently, just as he had done. "And thanks for the car. It's truly...luxurious."

"I knew you'd like it."

She saw him smile and felt his hand drift up her leg, fingers probing. Her right hand jumped again. This time it pushed his arm away and pointed down the street.

"Slow down, Eddie, there's the restaurant. See the valet parking?"

"La Fontaine? That's the restaurant? God, Toni, not another French restaurant. This time the menu better be in English."

"Oh, Eddie, don't worry...if it's in French, I'll translate for you." It might be a tiny matter, but tonight Eddie would have to depend on her if he wanted to eat. At least for a few hours she would have a little control, a little leverage, and that was something.

After Ruby polished the glass table and set out the platters of hors d'oeuvres, she tucked a single white blossom and one shiny leaf under each platter in the two o'clock position, exactly as Joyce Evans had directed. She placed small stacks of white cocktail napkins between the platters, pointing the corners toward the table edge. At one end of the table she arranged champagne glasses in two neat rows. Joyce instructed her to stand there and keep three or four glasses filled at all times.

At seven o'clock the gallery doors opened. The early visitors were quiet, well mannered. They admired the paintings, chatted with the artist, enjoyed the hors d'oeuvres and champagne. But later, when the crowd swelled, it occurred to Ruby that more people were interested in the refreshments than in the paintings.

She watched the artist, a homely young woman in a plain black dress, maneuver through the crowd to welcome two men from Channel 10 News. The cameraman seemed determined to capture the glamorous guests milling around the refreshment table, but the artist seemed just as determined to have him pan along the gallery walls where her paintings hung.

One elegantly dressed couple skirted the crowd and approached the table. Ruby heard the man say, "Thank heavens, it's real food. Do me a favor, Toni, and don't ever drag me to another French restaurant."

How handsome he was, Ruby thought, with that bad-boy look she always admired. The woman was handsome, too, fashionably dressed, her hairstyle elegant, her manicure perfect. Ruby paled, abruptly conscious of her own dull attire. Even the thought of her red lingerie failed to bolster her confidence. She looked around at the beautiful people, glamorous, laughing, carefree. She didn't belong here. She needed to leave. Panic surged up from her gut. She took a deep breath and pushed it back down.

"But the cassoulet was superb, Eddie. I enjoyed every bite," the woman replied, adjusting her shawl and looking over her shoulder.

Ruby exhaled sharply, then poured champagne into the next glass, concentrating on each detail of the bottle—its color, its heft, its chill—and watched the liquid bubble up in an arc within the glass. She hoped the distraction would trump the panic. Instead, she struggled for more air. Please, not now, she prayed.

The woman named Toni asked the man, "Did you notice the painting facing the front window, the young woman in the museum? The gold and scarlet would look fantastic in our dining room, don't you think? I wonder how much it is. I can't seem to find Joyce in this crowd. For goodness sake, Eddie, stop stuffing yourself. Oh, there she is! Come on, let's go ask her."

Ruby was breathing rapidly now. In another minute she'd have to run to the powder room in the hope that running water would drown out the sound of her gasping. But first she would make one more effort. She looked up from the table and focused her attention on the good-looking man who had turned back to nab another hors d'oeuvre. She concentrated on his lips, his jaw line. His mouth opened. Long, sure fingers popped a stuffed mushroom into it. His jaw closed, his fingers left his face.

And that's when it happened. A gun shot. Glass shattering. Another shot. The man falling! Screams.

Ruby stopped mid-breath and watched the crowd absorb the shock. The beautiful people, eyes opened wide and hands to their necks, inhaled a collective 'huh?' More than a few spilled their drinks. Across the table, the handsome woman in the shawl cried out "Oh, no!" and dropped to the floor, out of Ruby's view.

A deep voice behind her said something about a gift from Gordon—Ruby didn't catch the exact words. Before she could turn to look, an arm wrapped around her waist. A lean, muscular arm. The arm held her firmly, but not roughly, and slid upward, strong fingers cupping a breast. The same deep voice, this time close, clear and strong, said to the room, "Take it easy now. It's all over. No one else is gonna get hurt." Then softer, in her ear, "Come on, pretty lady, you're coming along with me. You're gonna get me out of town."

Out of town? His breath was soft and warm on her neck and when he spoke she felt his mouth move across her ear like a kiss. Yes, that's what he said, *out of town*. She was sure of it.

He stepped backward, pulling her with him. She took a slow, deep breath and leaned against his shoulder. Together they backed out the gallery door.

* * *

Had Ruby's mother been awake she would have seen what thousands of Channel 10 viewers saw that night: her daughter taken hostage, pulled from the crowd, her blouse open, a flash of red. She would have seen stuffed mushrooms on the polished floor and champagne dripping from the painting that the crowd, backing into the walls, had knocked crooked. According to the reporter, the gunman had accidentally put a bullet hole through a large painting hanging by the front window. The cameraman zoomed in for a better look and there was St. Agnes, shot through the neck, martyred once again. More importantly, the gunman had put a bullet into the man who was seen lying on the floor unconscious, shot in the groin. A beautiful woman in a crimson dress sat beside him, looking horrified and embarrassed by the nature of his injuries. Her black shawl lay like a dark jagged shadow across his hips, amputating his legs.

Channel 10 played the entire scene five times in succession. Each time the newscaster praised Channel 10's On-the-Scene-Team for its prompt response and accurate reporting, and each time identified the gallery, the hostage, the victim and the hospital, where his condition was reported as critical. The newscaster never mentioned the artist, who could be seen in the background straightening the paintings and waving at the camera.

Finally, after extensive interviews with a number of witnesses, the incident on Main Street was interrupted by a commercial. The increased volume caused Ruby's mother to wake up. It was almost ten, so she turned off the TV and went to bed.

BOHEMIAN RHAPSODY

Maria Grazia Swan

This time of the year night in the desert comes fast and cold. Restless in the leather seat of the Mercedes Benz, I drive and watch the shadows of dusk redefine the vanishing landscape. I hum with great determination but little conviction, trying to keep seeds of doubt from germinating in my brain.

"Too late, my time has come." Queen's lyrics spin in my head, over and over, useless as mother's milk to an aborted child. Still, I hum.

Cacti and tumbleweeds fly by and I fight the urge to floor the gas pedal, though the smoothness of the car on this barren road begs to be tested. It's going to be a long night.

"Do not attract attention." Pablo has warned me, forever and again. "Remember, we don't want to be noticed or questioned; that would be very unfortunate, a bad ending to our project." Over the phone, his voice sounded low and soothing. "I'll be waiting for you," added the skilled pretender with his weathered charm.

I wish I could pray. The way the nuns had taught me. *"Ave Maria, gratia plena . . ."* So long ago. I stopped praying after that first time, that first project. In my mind's eye I search for the face of the man, the faces of the others. Even now, months since we met her, an image of La Bowie's eyes flash in my head. From the moment I noticed her at the Malpensa airport in Milan, I'd felt funny. "Not funny, ha, ha," I had told Pablo. The kind of funny that's hard to define, the kind that puts a cramp in your bowels, like a painful menstruation. Except, this pain lasted much longer.

It had been during one of those union strikes Italians are known for. La Bowie was on her way out; we were on our way in. The three of us sat for hours on the tall stools at one of the bars at Malpensa, sipping cappuccino and bonding. We exchanged phone numbers. And glances.

Here we go again, I thought. Did Pablo notice her eyes? *Heterochromia iridis,* the David Bowie syndrome to us. Each eye a different color, like the English rocker. And so we tagged our new friend "La Bowie."

"The last one," Pablo had promised. At first I had assumed he would do it solo. A last encore before quietly retiring from the secluded resorts patronized by rich, lonely people. But he insisted I join him in the venture, and after weeks of bickering, I surrendered.

La Bowie lived in a small town in southern Arizona, United States. Her home, up a narrow, rocky road, was nice but not palatial. The house itself was at least 30 years old, with low ceilings and tiled floors. La Bowie called the floors *"saltillo."* She said it was a tile made by Mexican workers. It felt uneven under the feet, but also cool. There was a small pool and a gazebo. The grounds surrounding the home were landscaped with pebbles as small as the gravel used to cover graves in some European cemeteries. The vegetation had many thorns but little scent with the exception of a bed of gardenias she had planted on the north side of the house. La Bowie wasn't a native but could recite the names of plants such as desert spoon, octopus agave, chuparosa, and natal plum.

In the evening, the three of us would sit in the gazebo and watch the sun disappear into a bleeding sky. Oh, those sunsets were by far the most vibrant I have ever seen. And the nights were quiet but for the fronds of the tall palms. Their rustling and whispering brought back images of the orphanage's dark corridors with the rustle of nuns' habits and the whispers of forced prayers. Sometimes, the desert nights were broken by screams and howls of nocturnal creatures, waking me from my dreams, rekindling my concerns. I worried that the advances in forensic science and DNA testing would make things difficult, but for Pablo the risk added to the thrill. Was La Bowie worth the chance or was there something I didn't fully grasp? When I watched Pablo and La Bowie embrace I felt like a voyeur rather than an accomplice. I couldn't comprehend why. If their intimacy was the cause, was I jealous of him or her?

In the first five weeks I spent in La Bowie's home, no one came to visit. La Bowie's mail went to a rented postal box, and once a week, a large woman with dark shining hair came to clean and cook. She brought groceries from the nearby town. La Bowie left notes for the dark-haired woman and cash.

Pablo and La Bowie took frequent trips into the desert. Or so they said. Pablo would kiss "his little sister" on the cheek and off they went, for the rest of the day. I loved my time alone. That was my time for preparation, trying on La Bowie's clothes, making lists of cosmetics, personal items and perfecting the small things, like the way she folded sheets of paper before putting them in an envelope, or the way she hung a towel after a shower. That passion for details had kept me alive all these years. Me and Pablo. The drowning of Pablo's last wife had been ruled accidental because her grown children from her previous marriage had testified that their mother always folded her nightgown in a specific way and left

it on the edge of the pool before a night swim. Case closed.
The grieving young groom inherited the bulk of the estate.

I wandered from room to room under the scrutinizing
eyes of the cleaning woman. Servants are the best witnesses,
having one around at this stage of the project kept me alert. A
light scent floated in La Bowie's quarters, gardenia and
something else. I couldn't quite put a name to it. It just
smelled expensive and sophisticated. I made up my own label,
Essence of La Bowie. Once, I took one of her silky nighties and
slept in it. Coated in her scent, I felt happy and safe, even
alone in the big bed. It had been a long time since Pablo had
visited my room, and somehow, in this arid place, it didn't
matter. I did miss waking up to his laughter, his wanton
nakedness, and his ever present morning stiffness. But I
missed him a little less every day.

Soon I could move, speak, and laugh like La Bowie. I
could also forge her signature to perfection. Once that detail
had been conquered, I felt ready. Pablo, however, had many
excuses to postpone the final chapter. In the end he chose
"the boat scenario." Maybe it was sentimental, coming full
circle, that sort of thing. We started our career on the water,
and it appeared we would end it the same way. I referred to it
as "our nautical adventure," an expression I learned from La
Bowie. Pablo and La Bowie spent a weekend in San Diego
and purchased a pre-owned 30' Sea Ray at the yearly boat
show. La Bowie picked up the tab. I did not see the boat;
they had it towed directly to our offshore retreat. When Pablo
told me, I nearly blew our cover. How dare he? No one
besides the two of us had ever known of this special place. It
was our safe haven, our secret Shangri-La. I felt as if the place
had been desecrated, soiled.

Once again I asked myself "why?" How did La Bowie
get Pablo to do the unthinkable? Certainly not because of the
money. Over the years, we had completed countless projects
worth a lot more than La Bowie. At least I thought so.
However the extent of her financial worth remained
unknown; she didn't own companies or businesses. She had

never mentioned inheritance and didn't leave the house for extended periods of time, or if she did, it was with Pablo at her side. Where was her income coming from? She paid mostly with cash. There wasn't a safe anywhere in the house, her computer was outdated, and the only drawer she kept locked contained an average of $10,000 in cash at any given time, and bank statements from three different banks, all American, all with balances less than $20,000. One interesting thing that did come to light: she was a lot older than I had guessed. I decided not to tell Pablo about her age. Keeping that secret tasted more like revenge than caution. I told myself it was a girl thing. Love those Americanisms. All in all, La Bowie's lifestyle was uncomplicated and ordinary. Such flaunted conformity attracted me more than diamonds on platinum; what really hid underneath it all? I decided as soon as they were out of the way I would get to the truth, some way. In the meantime, I enjoyed the pool, the calm, and La Bowie's simple life in general.

One week after Pablo and La Bowie departed for their nautical adventure it was time to get to work. I left the letter and the cash for the cleaning lady, plus a fat severance bonus. No need to create negative feelings that might cause trouble later. Next I called La Bowie's doctor's office and in La Bowie's sweetest voice I convinced him to call in a prescription of Risperdal. I had to do a lot of improvising, describing imaginary symptoms, and hammering on the word; ASAP. I knew I sounded like her and finally convinced him I really, really, needed the medication. The prescription was called in, with refills. When each order was delivered from the pharmacy, I flushed the white oblong pills down the toilet and stashed the labeled, empty container in a safe place. No need to send traceable packages. Pablo had his own supply of Risperdal and the empty containers were enough to quell any questions should an autopsy show traces of the powerful antidepressant in La Bowie's system. I hoped she wouldn't suffer. I was entranced by her, and had slipped right into her skin. I wanted to know her better, share her thoughts, her dreams. I wanted to soak up her essence, discover the reason for my fascination with her.

By now her peaceful house up the rocky hill in that small southern Arizona town had exploded, painting the evening skies a deeper red than usual and erasing our tales of intrigue and betrayal.

I had spent too much time in that house: I knew every creaking hinge, every dripping faucet, and every crooked tile. I kept reminding Pablo of our mantra, *don't get too close to the subject, don't get too familiar with a location.* But I was the one who needed to remember. I watched a season change in La Bowie's home.

The new cleaning lady I hired had hair as dark and shining as the first one. She came to the house once a week, cooked and cleaned. I went to town to check my mail. I did everything like La Bowie. I was La Bowie.

Her income was still a mystery. Peculiarities surfaced the more I looked. The contents of her home were comfortable, but of little monetary value, easy to replace. It was the type of place you can leave with one or two suitcases and know nothing important is left behind. There was no remarkable art work, mostly copies, no family photos. She had no department store credit cards, and although she claimed only to speak English, books in French and Spanish were in her bedroom. Classics, mostly.

When I was bored I'd play "dress up" in her walk-in closet. This wasn't my first time, nor the first woman's closet. Pablo used to tease me and tell me it was the result of never having had toys or a mother when I was growing up. The teasing brought out my blushing bride routine. I'd take off my clothes slowly with lowered eyelids and a shy smile. In my remembrances of my best projects, we would end up on the closet floor and I would always be on top.

A pattern did emerge in La Bowie's banking history. Large deposits would show up on specific dates every two months. Each month the same amounts would be transferred from bank to bank, yet I couldn't pinpoint the origins.

According to the tax records, her house was owned by a corporation. I tried to follow the trail, but no such corporation existed in the state of Arizona. Since the house was earmarked for a burn, I let it go. The deeper I searched the less I found.

By now, Pablo and I only communicated by disposable cellular. He was still at our secret place, and while I was getting antsy and bored, Pablo wasn't budging. He said he needed more time, wasn't ready to move the boat. He never mentioned La Bowie, but I had images of their naked bodies, huddled on our luxurious Moroccan bed. I fretted. I sensed danger.

The day sky kept its stunning shades of blue, but the nights grew longer, and sometimes the wind from the desert circled the house, bringing a red dust that whipped the skin and burned the eyes. That same nameless wind would howl at night, tossing the lawn furniture and pushing branches against window panes. The isolation was getting under my skin.

It was the other morning, one of those windy days, when the deposit appeared in one of La Bowie's bank accounts. So many were the zeros in the amount that at first I laughed. A typo, I thought. As the smile on my face faded, I wondered what to do. I could research the maker of the deposit. I could call the bank to see if a mistake had been made. I could call Pablo and ask him what to do. In the past, that would have been my first move. I took a big breath, and with the click of a button, I moved the obscene amount of money from La Bowie's bank to my own private account. Yes! Now I laughed so hard that tears rolled into the keyboard and sat there.

When the house phone next to the computer rang, I jumped. "Unknown Name Unknown Number." I picked it up and whispered 'hello' in my best La Bowie sexy voice. By my second 'hello' the line was dead.

I had been the huntress for so long, and suddenly, I felt the hunted—and all it took was a phone hang up? That, and a very large sum of money. An unsettling coincidence. I sat in front of the computer for a long time. At dusk I decided to watch the news, to take my mind off the wind and the silent phone, but the windstorm had damaged the satellite and only 'snow' covered the screen. That night I woke in a cold sweat. Feeling jittery, I went to the bedroom window and strained my eyesight looking into the dark yard through cracks in the closed shutters. The fall moon rested in billowy dark clouds and all was still around the pool. Up by the gazebo, a moving shadow caught my attention. I held my breath and froze. I couldn't tell if it was a human or a beast, but it was big, moved slow and was now gone.

I fell to my knees incapable of thinking logically. My heart battered my chest with such loud thumping it seemed the walls of the house would reverberate and give away my presence to the outsider. Time passed, nothing happened. I didn't want to look outside again. When my breathing resumed its natural rhythm I crawled back into bed. In La Bowie's bed. My intuition told me there was a connection between the phone call, the money, and the shadow in the gazebo. And it was about La Bowie, or in this case, about me.

Was La Bowie afraid right now? Pablo always swore that our 'projects' never suffered. "They go to sleep," he'd say, "that's all. If they could talk they would tell you, it's the best way to go, no pain and in the arms of your loved one."

Pablo never used the words "death," or "dying." With him it was all so simple, so liberating. It was as if we performed them a favor, no, an act of kindness. Perhaps that's how Pablo and other masters of the dark, rationalize their deeds. To me, dark nights and suffering were soul mates into eternity.

Nights at the orphanage the old deacon would walk the aisle between our beds. In the dark, he stopped from time to time, slipping his rough hand under a blanket, searching, groping. We lay still, holding our breath, hoping he couldn't hear the clamor of our hearts. Praying he would move on. Prayers didn't work then, why would they now? Once he chose his prey, he would poke her awake with his walking cane, and it was over. His foul breath on your neck, his drunkard's voice would order you to his office. Trembling, in your bare feet, barely covered by a tattered nightie, you went. The walk back to the bed always faster, hurried. Pain shooting through you, your heart racing and your young mind fighting to control the rage of such an invasion of your body. After a while, the pain would go away, but the fear never did; it stayed with you every minute of every night. The old pervert was still there when I ran away from the orphanage.

Pablo found me on the beach. I had been trying to swim, wishing to drown. I, a pregnant twelve-year old runaway, he, a deck hand from the nearby Playa Hermosa Yacht Club. In his white uniform he appeared to me as an avenging angel. Surely he came to rescue me and punish the monster responsible. Punishment, I liked that word. I loved that idea: punish all bad people. Suddenly I knew—La Bowie's fortunes came from punishment. Blackmail. La Bowie blackmailed somebody, maybe more than one person. A corporation? Somebody who did bad things. That would explain the deposits showing up at precise dates, in specific amounts. Time after time. What a great way of making money, not hurting but making the bad ones pay. I felt liberated, no longer afraid.

Turning on all the lights as I moved through rooms, I went into the office, put "Bohemian Rhapsody" on, and sang along with Freddie: *"Because I'm easy come, easy go... Anyway the wind blows..."* I reexamined the bank books. No doubt. She was collecting from two different sources. Whichever had made the gargantuan deposit had to be extremely rich and extremely guilty. Also extremely angry. Probably the employer of the night caller. Hurray for La Bowie. I wished I could hug her, tell her how I admired her, longed to be like her. I pictured La Bowie punishing all the deacons of the word, all the perverts and child tormentors. A modern day Joan d'Arc of little orphans. But I couldn't hug her. Somewhere, far away, Pablo was popping Risperdal in her mouth, waiting for the perfect storm to take her out to sea in her damaged Sea Ray. *"Mama, ooo, Didn't mean to make you cry."* I sang and I cried, for Freddie, long gone, for La Bowie, on her way out, and mostly for myself, caught in this landslide with nowhere to run.

In the morning sunlight everything looked different. The gazebo was the same except for a cigarette butt left on the ground. Time to move on, with or without Pablo. I didn't know if the night intruder had come for me or La Bowie. It didn't matter. We were one. The cleaning lady wasn't due for two more days. I began my last chore. Room by room, meticulously shifting through everything, deciding what had to be taken and what would be left behind. Once that was done, I did it again, and again, until the 'take' pile easily fitted the trunk of the car. Greed did not promote survival. La Bowie had left very little to be packed.

One small detail troubled my mind. Her paper shredder had been emptied but for some strips, larger than normal, at the very bottom. The paper was old, yellowish, and the type used for official documents, handwritten, not in English. I tried to match the pieces together to read it, but it was difficult to see and time was running short. Numbers? Dates? One word I recognized: Hermosa. Hermosa as in Playa or as an adjective? Had I been set up? Did Pablo and La Bowie know each other before the encounter in Italy? If they had left me behind to take the wrath for her blackmailing, the joke was on them. The money had been safely transferred, and not even Pablo knew of my private offshore account.

By early afternoon everything was set. The fire accelerant was in the kitchen, a trail of fabric softener sheets lay from the kitchen to the entryway, all was ready to go. I took my last stroll around what felt like home. Should have never spent so much time in the same place. It really was like saying goodbye to my own house except, I had never had a house, had never belonged anywhere. We lived like gypsies. *Bohemians* of the world, Pablo liked to call us. How would he handle this? He didn't know I was leaving. I didn't care that he didn't. I lit the match, put it to the first sheet and made sure it began to smolder. It would be hours before the sheets in the kitchen ignited the accelerant and caused the explosion. By then I'd have crossed the border. I put out the match, slipped it in my pocket, got in La Bowie's Mercedes and left without looking back.

The road in front of me is narrow and dark, stones skitter under my tires. Far on the horizon, lightning flashes. The perfect storm is brewing; Pablo's prediction is coming to pass. One hill away from the water I roll down my window and inhale, hoping to smell the brine. I smell dust and rain. I ditch all evidence in a trash can at a rest stop just outside Arizona. Crush the now useless cell phone with a rock before disposing of it. It feels good, almost. Except I don't want to think about La Bowie, her eyes still crowd my mind. I look into the rearview mirror and the irises of my eyes, in the deceptive glow of the dashboard, look the same color. For tonight I'm like everyone else, no *Heterochromia iridis*. I smile at the optical illusion. It will last until dawn.

I park the car at the top of the hill and walk down to the small, deserted beach where the Sea Ray is anchored by large protruding boulders. At least I hope it is the Sea Ray. Pablo must have moved the boat to the shore from our hideaway. Good. Could he have known I was coming? I hear the creaking of planks, as the boat rocks in the rising, angry sea. Only two lights are on. A thunderbolt lights the sky, and I see a silhouette on the deck. Fear finds me again, cold beads of sweat tunnel down my spine. Did he see me? Did he recognize me? I wish I had a gun. Does he know my intentions? I stand for awhile. The wind's furor grows, and I know time has run out.

I walk, I can no longer see the silhouette. Huge waves crash on the rocks and against the boat. The sky changes colors faster than fireworks and paints the foamy waters in many shades of black. I want to do something, but I don't know what. I wish I could die, no, go to sleep, like Pablo said, go to sleep in the arms of my loved one. I step into the water, and walk toward the Sea Ray through churning, foaming currents. The water is cold on my ankles. Cold on my bare legs. The boat seems unreachable and I realize it isn't just rocking, it is moving. Moving away. I panic, open my mouth to scream, but there is no one to hear me.

I stand there, and the water is mounting and I don't know what to do, where to go. The salty wetness on my cheeks is part salt water and part tears. Crying for what, for whom? I watch the Sea Ray growing smaller or maybe it is an illusion created by the storm. The water is up to my knees, to my thighs, I'm clutching my purse, with the car keys and the false documents for two. Is this all there is left? Where did I go wrong? Pablo. I open my mouth to call his name, but my lips whisper "La Bowie." Strong fingers grasp my shoulder and I don't move. I'm too tired to fight back. *He knew, he was waiting for me.* I hold the purse against my chest. *Go to sleep in the arms of your loved one.* Nice story. I remember that prayer now: *Ave Maria, gratia plena, Dominus tecum.* I recite it as I turn, slowly, ever so slowly. The sea roars and the sky burns and I smell gardenia. My face brushes the collar of a wet raincoat. "Glad you made it, little orphan," whispers La Bowie. "Did you find the fire accelerant in the kitchen?"

I nod, my head resting against her bosom. I look back to the sea, where the boat was anchored, "Pablo?" I ask.

"Taken care of," she says, not a trace of Risperdal slur in her voice.

"Mama, just killed a man
Put a gun against his head"

"Shall we go?" I hand her the keys to the car. "You drive, I have had a long ride." We hike up the muddy hill in the pouring rain, and I swear I can hear her humming "Bohemian Rhapsody."

FAST PACE

Robin Merrill

I saw the drug deal go down while doing 3.8 mph at a 5% incline. The heart monitor registered 148, a perfect rate for the transition coming up. I kept the pace rocking to the rhythm in the headphones, and watched two men talking in the parking lot.

For me, the view out the small windows spaced along the curve of the building was usually more interesting than the TV monitors attached above them. The juts and peaks of the bare McDowell Mountains, the dancing landscape foliage and occasional wildlife appealed more than silent newscasts and sports clips. Especially when the wildlife was two-legged, male, and clad in shorts and cutaway muscle shirts.

Prime view, I thought, and enjoyed a bonus for forty-five minutes on the treadmill.

The last drum rolls thundered through my bones. I punched down the incline and breathed deeply, kicking up the speed to 4.2 when the next tune exploded and my legs caught the fast pace.

The men were still talking when I checked the view again. Friends, I figured, or workout buffs getting acquainted after sweating together. I'd seen the dark one before, lifting the heavy weights at machines I stayed far away from. He was pleasant to the men and kept an eye to the women.

Now if my guy were more pleasant, I wouldn't mind at all. I didn't even know his name. He never spoke, never smiled, never came on to me. But he looked. The guy fried my circuits with his looks when he first spotted me as we went about our routines. And then he ignored me. Despite kicking myself and questioning my sanity, I kept going out of my way to provide that first look. Some day, one of us might do something about it.

I thought the men were leaving when the stranger walked away, but he went to a screaming lemon-yellow Hummer, got a small package, and returned. He carried it by the yarn handles, a charming froufrou gift bag a woman would use for a casual token. I smiled, tickled by the picture he made.

His friend didn't look inside. He folded it into a small bundle, slipped something to the guy, and within seconds they split, the stranger to the ridiculous Hummer, the dark-haired hunk to a sedate BMW.

Could that be what it looked like? At 6:15 a.m. in a Scottsdale gym?

I gripped the heart monitor strips and let the scene replay. Of course, there could be a ton of innocent explanations. But what if I'd just seen a drug deal happen in front of my very own eyes? My heart rate read 156, but I knocked a couple of points off for excitement, lowered the incline, and finished the workout.

I knew who to talk to.

By the time I met Mark Brewer for lunch at Houston's three days later, I'd about shrugged it off, except that I'd seen the hunk again at the gym, and an uneasy feeling nagged at me.

Mark and I go back a few years. He was married to a friend of mine, and when she bailed, we saw one another socially. We remained stuck at friends, though, which was just as well.

He's a Scottsdale cop, and sometimes I have a problem with authority.

When I told Mark the story, it didn't sound as funny as I'd hoped it would. At least, he didn't laugh. "Did you get the license plates?"

"No," I said, "I didn't think it was a big deal."

"You see a possible drug deal and it's no big deal?"

His cop suspicions seemed much harsher than mine. "Probably just pot. So what? Somebody smokes a little in their own damn home."

He lowered the gigantic burger. "It's the law, Kathy. You know, those civilized rules I'm sworn to uphold."

"Yeah, yeah. Look, I don't want you to make some schmuck's life miserable over a little marijuana, but...what if it's something else?"

His eyes gleamed at me. "So you *do* want me to do my job for some things, heh?"

I gave him a look. He took me over the details and descriptions a few times, but he didn't treat it like a big deal, either.

So I forgot about it.

I watched my guy park his cobalt truck near the same spot every day. Right in front of the treadmills. Whether warming up for weights, or doing distance, I watched him lock his sexy trunk and saunter in. And every time I wondered why he was so damn intriguing.

He continued to work out with his two buddies, send me intense looks and pretend I didn't exist. I checked for a ring. He didn't have one. I watched to see if he liked the scantily-clad goddesses who did power lifts. He didn't bat an eye.

I worked up to a smile. He nodded. The next day he said, "Morning," as I walked past his weight station and my heart tripped. A tenor. I'd expected something else. His single earring glittered; his dark eyes remained straight and sober. He wasn't handsome, wasn't the fittest or youngest around. But he had something that sang to me.

"Morning," I said, and kept walking.

Progress! Jeeze, what now?

That night Mark was killed.

The news hit me in the face over coffee. I finished *The Arizona Republic* article, sat at the office breakroom table and wept. Two reported details haunted me. He'd been on duty, and a witness thought she saw a yellow vehicle near the scene of the shooting. Mark accepted a cop's risks, but I knew in my heart he'd been following up on my story, and the pain slashed deep.

I spent the evening talking to myself. Sometimes I paced, sometimes I threw myself on the bed. It didn't matter. I couldn't change what had happened, and I couldn't figure out what to do.

Go to the police? Fine. And tell them what? Look for a yellow Hummer because something I said got Mark killed?

Puffy-eyed and exhausted, I went to the gym the next morning. I wanted to look for the hunk. Maybe I could get some information, something the police would have to listen to.

I didn't know I needed to see my guy until he wasn't there. It hit me hard, and then I pretended I didn't care. I recited 'I like living alone. I don't need anyone' with each lift. The weights grew extra lead. I pushed the reps hard. Sweat splattered the bench beneath my face as I completed the last set of kneeling arm curls.

When I stood, there he was.

My heart leaped. Thank God, he's here, I thought. Maybe if he hadn't been looking at me, I could have recovered and ignored him as usual. But to my embarrassment, my face crumpled and the tears started. I jerked away, left the weight on the bench, and took off.

I got to the door before I heard his tenor voice ring out. "Hold on." I didn't slow down. "Hey, wait just a minute."

I shoved the door open and was a couple strides outside when he grabbed my arm and spun me around. My shock and my pride had me struggling to control my face.

He gripped both arms and studied me with those dark eyes, intense and up close. He wasn't ignoring me now. "I know something's wrong. I couldn't let you leave hurting like that. Can I help?"

I needed the comfort of his arms more than I'd needed anything in my life, so I held myself rigid. "No...I...thank you. It's just...a friend was killed the other day, and when I saw you...I mean...thanks."

His hands eased, slid up and down and released me. The loss of contact struck like a shaft of ice into my heart. Alone and isolated, I stood two feet from my fantasy guy and might as well have been in another universe.

I started to turn away.

"Don't go," he said, aborting a hand movement when I stopped.

My eyes found his, and then welled over. I managed little more than a whisper. "I don't even know your name."

A tiny smile touched his lips. "Rick. Rick Eliot."

When I stood there, blinking, he asked, "And yours?"

Oh. "Kathy. Kathy Bartell." My mind was gone. Totally gone.

"Was he a...good friend?"

"Yes. Yes, I think he was." Then my brain kicked in. We were out of sync, doing the meet and greet while I was tied in knots over Mark.

Life can suck.

"Not more than friends. It's just that I got him killed..." I couldn't do this. I pivoted to take off again and got one step.

"Whoa, now. Hold on, Kathy, just take it easy."

He had me around the shoulders, pulled back against his body. I bit my lip, hard, to keep the shudders hitting me from migrating to full-scale waterworks. Somehow, he knew enough to let me fight it out. His arms held tight, his face pressed against my head, his voice spouting nonsense, but he let me settle before loosening his hold.

Too messed up for modesty, I lifted the hem of my tee shirt and wiped my face. I don't cry well. I faced him anyway.

After a pause, he asked, "Will you stay here while I get my keys? We'll get a coffee or coke and talk."

The last thing I wanted was to be with my guy like this. On a scale of 1 to 10, the romance factor was about −15. I nodded.

"Promise?"

I hesitated. My keys were inside, but I could walk home in ten minutes.

I nodded again.

He took me straight to Starbucks, which normally would have been a sign from heaven. After I cleaned up and sipped my latté, I relaxed enough to look at him. Rick. My guy was named Rick. I smiled into his sober midnight eyes and had to blink again.

"Sorry."

"No problem. Will you tell me about it?"

I nodded, and swiped my face. Rick had gotten a wad of napkins, and he handed me one. Smart man. I like a man who thinks ahead.

"My friend, Mark, he's...he was a cop..."

"Mark Brewer?"

"Yes," I said, unsurprised, as it'd been in the news, and told him the entire story. His eyes never left my face, but I couldn't keep contact. My fingers kept folding and refolding the napkin. I'd studied this guy for months, fantasized about him, absorbed him. The attraction, the connection, was there, but I didn't know him.

"I looked for the hunk this morning, but he wasn't at the gym. When I find him, I'll..."

"Stop right there." His hand snaked out to cover mine. He wasn't gentle.

"You will not find this hunk. You will not talk to him. You will not even look at him. Do you understand?"

I tried to pull back. "No, I don't understand! It's my responsibility to..."

His hand tightened and he leaned forward. "No, it's not. It's the police's responsibility, not yours. You stay out of it."

"I don't see any police around here, do you? If you think..."

"Yes, I do see the police. Or rather, I am the police."

I shut my mouth. My eyes took their time, tracking his entire face, as his did the same to mine. Whatever attracted me poured out of his eyes, his being. Like an addict, I drank him in. It wasn't enough.

"This isn't fair." My voice was ragged, almost hoarse. "I don't even *like* cops."

He laughed. When he leaned closer, I knew the smell of him.

"Yes, you do."

So now I had a date with my guy. I met him two hours later at the police station, to fill out paperwork and look at mug shots. Lucky me. An officer took me back to the squad room where Rick stood with his tall workout buddy. After one of his intense looks, he said, "Clem, Kathy Bartell. Howard Clements."

His friend grinned and shook my hand. "Call me Clem."

"The other fellow, is he a cop, too?"

Rick shifted beside us. I'd gone back to practicing ignoring him. I'd gotten so good at it I didn't want to lose my edge. I wasn't convinced a cop would work for me, especially this one. Once he got rolling, he did authority with a vengeance.

"Naw. Joe's a stockbroker," Clem said.

"That's a relief."

The whole of Clem's dark, homely face was consumed by his laughter. Rick shot him a laser beam look.

I got through the ordeal. No mug shots popped. The primary on Mark's case conducted the interview. She was good, patient when it got hard, respectful with my story, and she didn't make me feel like a heel for not coming in sooner. Of course, I could probably thank my guy Rick for that.

I didn't hang around.

My day brightened when I spotted the hunk shopping for groceries at AJ's. I didn't think of Rick's instructions earlier that morning. Why should I? If I had, I wouldn't have stopped. I wasn't too happy with authority right then.

But I might've been cleverer about it.

I caught up with him between the melons and tomatoes. "Hi." I grabbed a package of vine-ripened cherry tomatoes. "Haven't I seen you at Maximum Fitness?"

He jolted and dropped his fruit into the display case. An ocean of oranges started to shift forward towards the floor and his hands stemmed the tide in first one place and then another, until the wave of sliding oranges subsided. He straightened, red faced and awkward.

"Uh, no, I don't think so," he mumbled, glancing at me and turning away. "Sorry." He put a couple oranges into his basket and moved off.

He lied. A hunk in shorts is still a hunk in regular clothes. And I did look at faces, too. His matched.

I followed, carrying my tomatoes. "I'm sure I saw you there last week. Was it Monday? Yeah, Monday." I wanted to add, *When you were talking with the yellow Hummer creep, remember?* But I wasn't totally stupid.

"No, no. You're mistaken." His eyes were wild, his face pale. He abandoned the basket and headed out.

Well, come on. If I'd been hitting on him, would a reasonable man have been that scared of me? Not until they knew me, I decided, and figured I was on to something.

I hit the parking lot about sixty feet behind him and losing ground. If I'd had more time I could have done a stroll towards an imaginary car, but he didn't give me that luxury. Since I wanted the license plate, I had to run.

The black BMW backed out of the slot and headed for the Frank Lloyd Wright exit. I stood in the lane, and tried to see the letters and numbers until it squealed around the end row. Damn, damn, damn. What the hell good are glasses if you can't see? I got 213A, and lost the last two letters. Or maybe it was 218. The A was pretty easy because of its shape. I repeated it until I got it written down and went back inside to think things over.

Did the gym get car information when people registered? I couldn't remember. I'd joined a couple of years before, when I moved to North Scottsdale after my divorce. They're computerized. We use a barcode strip to check in on a magnetic scanner, and I've seen client records on screen. I'd think of a ploy in the morning to read mine.

Then I could maybe…well, of course the cops would be looking at Monday's records. Wouldn't they? I'd have to ask my guy. They could narrow it down by time.

Their search should be a slam-dunk.

I watched Rick back into his favorite slot and my heart went to mush. I was going to have to work harder at ignoring this guy if I wanted to avoid more complications than I needed in my life. I'd done difficult relationships.

No more.

But I liked being greeted by smiles from the three musketeers when our paths crossed. Better than a cold shoulder any day. Rick scorched me with his eyes, and then went silent. I met Joe. Clem did the intro. He was a fount of friendship compared to the cops. I eased away. I had a routine to finish.

"Wait for me up front," Rick said. I looked, but his face was unreadable. Fine by me. I wanted some answers.

I saw the cop in him when he came out of the shower room, now that I knew. Good cheer was not native to his face. But I saw a hunger and need in those eyes, the tiny gold hoop in his right ear and thought of the sexy cobalt truck; somehow a cheery face didn't matter one iota. I saw deeper into the man than the surface. I just wasn't pleased about it.

"I'll walk you to your car," he said, and we walked.

Recalling his rude instructions, I broke the silence on the offensive. "I've got a partial license number for the hunk. It's…"

"Where'd you see a license plate?" He crowded me against the car.

"Where'd you lose your manners?" I shoved him back. "And stop interrupting me. You listen to what I have to say or we don't talk at all. Got that?"

His lips suggested a curve, and a sparkle lit his eyes. "Yeah. Sorry, bad habit." His eyes locked with mine until I flushed and looked away. Jeeze. He could melt an ice bank.

The back of his hand brushed my cheek. "Okay, you were explaining where you saw the license plate."

"Not exactly," I said, trying to settle my heart. "I was going to give you a partial number."

"Give me both."

I knew he wouldn't like it, but I told him, and waited for the explosion.

He studied me in silence. My eyes found lots of things to watch besides his face. "Let me get this straight. First, you let the guy know you saw him the day of the drug deal. Then you run into the parking lot and stand there looking, so he knows you're suspicious and had just tagged him. That about sums it up?"

I cleared my throat. I couldn't do anything about the red face. "Pretty much."

"Right." He could've been discussing the lack of rain, except for the hard glint in those eyes. "I suppose it's useless to tell you how stupid it was to move on this guy, or that you did exactly what I told you not to do?" He spit the last part out with precision.

I wanted to squirm, so I squared my stance and looked him dead in the eye.

"Yes, I'd say so." And wet my lips.

He sat his bag on my trunk, moving slowly, giving me all the time in the world to freak out about it, gripped my shoulders, brought his body against mine and kissed me brainless.

I may have started late, but I caught up. When he stepped back, I had to unlock my hands from his back, and his breathing was as ragged as mine. Shoving his hands in his pockets, he stared at me, the planes of his sober face fierce.

"See you tomorrow," he said, grabbed his bag and walked away.

Well. I guess he showed me. The guy had a "me Tarzan, you Jane" attitude a mile wide. But being Jane felt pretty good right then. I wondered if that was the biggest weapon Tarzan had: Jane's built-in Trojan horse.

As I unlocked my Acura, I realized I hadn't asked my questions, and I wasn't about to now. I'd have to come up with answers on my own.

During my lunch break, I went back to the gym to talk to the desk jockey. I was in luck. Alan, the regular morning person, was still on. I got my answers. They didn't record license information, and the police had been around asking about a yellow Hummer and copying the files. The records showed check-in time, but when he told me they had about forty to sixty people come through that early, I wasn't sure finding the creeps would be a slam-dunk.

Discouraged, I started to leave but thought of another ploy. "What's with the yellow Hummer? Thought I saw it here and I just love it."

Alan grinned. "Pretty wild, heh? Guy hangs around sometimes. I forgot to tell the cops I saw him coming out of

Fountain Hills awhile back, though. Don't see many Hummers that color."

I wanted to call Rick a dozen times, but I wouldn't take that step. Even though it was police business and the right thing to do for Mark, calling him was too personal. I didn't think to call Detective Martinez, Mark's primary. Right or wrong, Rick was my cop. My guy. I had some things to straighten out first, that was all.

And one of those things was Rick Eliot.

That night I drove out to Fountain Hills. I told myself there were no risks. Besides, what were the odds of actually finding a Hummer on the street? People in Fountain Hills had more garages than most people had bedrooms.

But I could look.

I didn't know which of the three entrances Alan meant. There were plenty of homes sprawled over those hills. I took the first, Palisades Boulevard, with its horse-named streets and gated communities I could only drift past in frustrated speculation. The next, Fountain Hills Boulevard, had more ungated homes, more streets. I kept driving in the dark. If a yellow Hummer was sitting outside, I figured it'd glow in my headlights. Nothing. I went on.

Saguaro Boulevard, the oldest and most developed, defeated me. Two hours I spent looking, and I covered about half. I saw Hummers. Three of them, parked in driveways. None were yellow. I wondered what they had in the garages to leave a Hummer orphaned. But I did narrow the probable target area.

I'd try again tomorrow.

Relieved it was a treadmill day and less opportunity to run into my guy, I did my time, shirt soaked with the effort. Then I snuck the long way around the central equipment sections and headed for the door.

"Kathy!"

Busted. I got my keys off the board and turned to a scowling Rick.

"Hi." I smiled.

He didn't. He was still in his gym clothes, arms and face gleaming. "Going somewhere?"

"Well, yeah. To work." That sounded good, didn't it?

"Let's step outside." He took me by the arm. It wasn't meant to be a courtesy, but a come-along.

Evidently, not good enough. Soon as we were outside, I started in. "Look…"

He didn't release me. "Something's going on. What're you up to?"

"Nothing!"

His voice softened, and his hands touched me, caressing my shoulders. "Talk to me."

I caved, and told him about searching for the Hummer.

He looked up and addressed the Divine Being. "I knew you were messing with me!"

"What do you mean?"

"I held out as long as I could." His eyes racked over my face, down my body. "I knew you'd be trouble. Nobody looks like you without being trouble for someone." His face came closer. "God help me, but it looks like I'm your someone, lady, so you listen to me."

I couldn't speak. My hands crushed my MP3 player and towel against my wet shirt. Somewhere in there I detected a compliment, and that was crazy. Had this man ever seen me in anything but sweat, gym clothes, and a 6 a.m. face and hair? Oh, yeah. Once. At the police station.

"Stay away from Fountain Hills, stay away from license plates, and stay out of police business, do you hear?" He punctuated each couplet with a shake.

I blinked, trying to keep back the tears. Angry tears. I wouldn't admit to the hurt. "Maybe I'd just better stay away from you."

His hands clenched tight, then he slid then up to capture my face, his fingers buried in my soaking wet hair. "Not a chance."

This time he didn't linger; he didn't finesse. He branded me with a kiss, and walked back into the gym without a word.

I would have told him about my plan if he'd been reasonable about the whole deal. But since he was too busy being macho Rick, I showered, called in some time off, and went back to Fountain Hills. Twenty minutes later, I found a yellow Hummer.

I stopped dead in the street, heart clamoring like a gong.

I fumbled in my purse for my PDA, punched the license number in, threw it in the passenger seat and hightailed it down the street, half laughing, half crying. "Got you now, you bastard!"

Swinging around the corner, my heart stuttered. There was another yellow Hummer. "Shit."

License recorded, I set out again, considerably more subdued. Who would have figured? I went on with my street scanning, growing more discouraged as two more Hummers turned up, neither one yellow. There were too many Hummers, too many homes, too many...

Another yellow Hummer, backed into the driveway, the rear license plate close to the garage door, the front an Arizona Suns banner.

I drove on past and almost kept going. What use was this fool's errand? I didn't want to get out, but I couldn't give up. I turned around and checked out the house. Nothing moved, nothing wiggled. I parked across the street and with my PDA open in my sweaty hand, I got out and inspected the house, studied the PDA, crossed the street, and did the same thing. The stylus slipped in my shaky fingers as I made graffiti notes and emanated real estate agent for all I was worth. I looked around, walked to the back of the Hummer. The plate was almost pressed against the garage door.

I'd just entered the number into the PDA when the front door opened.

"Hey, what the hell are you doing?"

I should have tried a yellow-Hummer-fan ploy. Looking for my dog. Anything.

I ran.

He caught me before I reached my car door. When I turned to fight, he slugged me. My head crashed into the car. I blacked out for a few moments. He had me about the torso dragging me up the sidewalk like a sack of dog food when I surfaced.

I tried to yell.

He clamped a hand over my mouth.

I'm strong, I thought, and tried to struggle. That didn't work, either.

The creep was 6' 2" or 3", and built like a shithouse. He had me inside and thrown on the floor with one knee crushing my chest before I had a chance to pray.

"You're the bitch who followed Henderson, aren't you?"

I'd never seen a person come close to the animal viciousness unleashed on me now. Death snarled inches from my face. The smell of fear rose from my skin.

"I...I...don't know what you're talking about. I...I was looking at the...the...yellow Hummer. I work for a builder, and I was here on bu...business. I swear."

The slap jarred my brain and bloodied my lips. "You ran."

"You...you scared me. You came after me fir...first."

His knee eased up. Maybe he was buying it. I kept talking. "I've got business cards. If you'd let me up..."

"Shut up."

I did, because he was thinking, instead of attacking.

"Shit, first the cop and now you. What a fucking mess."

He wrapped my wrists and ankles together with duct tape, and gagged me with it. I lay on a bed, alone, battered, waiting for the worst. The chemical smell of the tape near my nose sickened me. Keeping my stomach calm so I wouldn't vomit was one of my big worries for the first hour. Holding my bladder so I wouldn't pee my pants occupied the second and third hours.

When the crashing and shouting started, despair filled me. I thought the thugs were battling it out. Gunshots peppered the general chaos. Then the silence built like a toothache, until the door bashed into the wall.

Two men leaped into the room, but I saw only my guy, his gun in his hand and his eyes burning into mine.

I listened to the harangue until Rick began to repeat himself. "Hardheaded woman. I told you to stay out of it!"

"You could've told me you were on to the creep!" I winced as his fingers probed my jaw, and slapped at his hand.

"His name's Jeff Rutledge, and you could've minded your damn business and let us do our job!" His bloodied handkerchief wiped my face again. I lay locked against him with one arm, where I'd been since he cut the tape.

He angled his head towards the door and hollered. "Where's the damn medic?"

Clem appeared. "They'll be a few minutes. Still working on Rutledge." His eyes gleamed. "Don't worry, he'll live," he said, and disappeared.

Great news. The creep would pay for Mark.

Rick concentrated on mangling the cloth in his hand. When he looked up, his expression was bleak, his voice gone quiet. "I didn't know you were here until I saw your car. Jesus, Kathy, my heart stopped. Clem…Clem saved me from making an ass of myself. If you'd been dead or seriously hurt…"

"I wasn't." My hand cupped his cheek. "I'm okay."

"No thanks to me. You're right. I should've kept you in the loop. Maybe you'd have stayed out of trouble." His smile was bent, but willing.

"Maybe."

That night, stiff, sore and turning purple, my fantasy world started coming true. My guy asked me out to dinner.

Life can be good.

IN MEMORY OF MAGGIE

Susan Budavari

Before reaching the waiting area for her eight-fifty flight from Newark to Phoenix, the shapely young woman with long, black hair stopped, pushed onto her tiptoes and hugged her brother. "Thanks, Tommy." She took a deep breath. "Wish me luck."

"Any second thoughts, Rayna?"

She shook her head.

"Okay." He glanced at his watch. "Your flight will board any minute. Everything's taken care of."

"Brenda?"

"She'll find you in Phoenix." He took hold of her hands for a brief moment. "Just remember Maggie." He turned and walked away.

Rayna lifted the straps of her denim overnight bag onto her shoulder then tugged at her orange spandex tee-shirt to cover up the exposed skin above her size-three jeans. Several eyes followed her as she made her way to the line forming at the gate.

* * *

Rayna maneuvered around people edging her way down the crowded center aisle of the plane. She dragged her bag which felt heavier each moment. After enduring two unexplained delays in boarding, she was anxious to get to her seat and on her way.

She felt a flutter in her stomach when she reached her row and caught the eye of the pudgy, middle-aged man in a golf cap seated on the aisle. Rayna pointed to the window seat to let him know it was hers. The man whispered in the ear of the slender-faced blonde in dark glasses seated next to him.

Rayna searched for room in the overhead bin for her bag. Her first two attempts to squeeze the bag in were unsuccessful, and she struggled to keep it from falling. She apologized when her foot brushed the foot of the man in the aisle seat.

"Let me give you a hand with that," he offered.

She gave him a grateful smile as she stepped aside.

Several inches taller than Rayna, he easily moved the contents of the bin around and stowed her bag. "That'll do it." He closed the overhead door, then leaned over to speak to the blonde in the middle seat. "Carrie, you'll have to come out now. The girl who has the window seat is ready to get in."

She stood and inched her way out. Rayna slid in and sat down.

After they fastened their seat belts, the woman spoke to Rayna.

"I hope we'll take off soon."

Rayna looked at her watch and nodded. "We're over an hour late already."

The woman whispered, "I hope there's nothing wrong. I get nervous every time they delay a flight."

"If anything were wrong, they'd have changed planes."

"My name's Carrie Mitchell and the big guy next to me is my husband." She nudged him. "We just spent a week in New York and are heading home."

He leaned toward Rayna and clasped her hand, "Evan Mitchell. Call me Evan."

"I'm Rayna." She blushed when Evan held onto her hand too long and she had to disengage it.

"Evan said you're about our daughter's age. He thinks you look like a dancer."

Rayna chuckled. "Good guess." It was clear to Rayna from Carrie's movements she was blind. Rayna wondered if she should say something but decided to see if it came up in their conversation.

"We swapped seats so another couple could sit close to friends. Now I'm glad we did. Talking to you is much better than being squeezed between two big guys who'd elbow me the whole flight."

"Please, let me know if I bother you." Rayna leaned back in her seat and closed her eyes waiting for take-off.

Once they were safely in the air, Carrie patted Rayna's arm. "Do you live in Phoenix?"

"New Jersey. In New Providence."

"We're originally from Summit. We could've passed each other on the road . . . at one time."

"Where do you live now?"

"Scottsdale."

" Do you like Arizona?"

"Love it. But I still have trouble when it goes above 110 in summer." Carrie reached into her purse for a tissue. She took off her dark glasses, blotted her eyelids and put the glasses back on.

"I'm planning to move to Prescott. It doesn't get to 110 there, does it?"

"Rarely." She waited a moment, then added, "Why Prescott? Do you have family there?"

"No."

"Why, then?"

"It's a beautiful place—small now, but taking off. Lots of opportunity. Do you ever get up there?"

"No. We don't drive around much these days. I can't." She laughed. Then she whispered, "And Evan's license is suspended."

"Oh." Rayna wasn't going to pursue that subject.

"Staying long in Phoenix?"

"Just overnight. I'm off to Prescott in the morning."

"I suppose you're staying with friends."

"No, I'll get a hotel room."

"Oh, dear. It'll be pretty late when we get in. You're going to look for a room then?"

"Uh huh. I was told I shouldn't have a problem."

"If you were my daughter, I'd worry."

"I'll be careful."

Carrie turned to her husband and said, "Rayna's moving to Prescott."

He craned his neck to look straight at Rayna. "You must be excited about starting a new life there."

Rayna nodded and smiled, letting him continue.

"You get to make a fresh start. Nobody will know you." Evan had a faraway look in his eyes.

"Would you like to do that?" Rayna grinned.

"What?"

"Start over again."

"Me, no." Evan shook his head. "Been there. Did that five years ago—Carrie and I moved to Arizona. I wanted to make it big in golf." He sighed. "It hasn't happened yet."

Rayna studied his face. As she opened her mouth to speak, the flight attendant reached their row with the beverage cart and offered drinks. Carrie asked for tea, Rayna a diet soda, and Evan ordered a double scotch. He sipped his drink and turned away while the women continued their conversation.

"I would imagine there's not much for dancers up in Prescott," Carrie remarked.

"There you go." Rayna smiled. "That's an opportunity."

Carrie chuckled. "You sound like my daughter—always looking at the bright side. I like that."

The two women chatted over the next hour. Rayna heard that Evan worked as a golf instructor but was "down on his own game," and Carrie had been a teacher prior to the accident that claimed her sight. Carrie did most of the talking. She asked few questions of Rayna, which was a relief to her.

The second time the flight attendant passed by with the beverage cart, Evan ordered another double scotch. He glanced at Rayna and smiled. "Can I get you something?" She politely refused.

Evan scowled at the attendant when she hesitated to serve him. He raised his voice. "What are you waiting for?"

As soon as the attendant was out of ear shot, Carrie apologized to Rayna for Evan's outburst and mentioned his penchant for alcohol. Quietly, she said, "I'm really sorry for talking your ear off."

"No problem, really. I'm enjoying your company." Rayna excused herself and got out to go to the lavatory. When she returned, she found Carrie and Evan with their heads together whispering.

When they were all seated again and buckled in, Carrie said, "Our daughter's at college in Tucson and her room's empty. Why not stay with us tonight? You won't have to look for a room and it'll save you some money. "

"That's kind of you, but I can't impose." She thought for a few moments. "Do you think I'll have a problem finding a room?"

"Probably not, unless it's very late when we get in. Anyway, the offer stands. Think about it."

"Thanks, I will."

"I'll leave you alone now, dear. I'm going to try to sleep for a while."

"Sleep sounds like a great idea," Rayna responded. She closed her eyes.

* * *

Rayna and the Mitchells deplaned together and walked toward the Baggage area. Rayna noticed that Evan stumbled along the way and slurred a few of his words. When she asked him if he was okay, he boasted, "I'm perfectly fine." He wrinkled up his face and added, "Even if I can't walk straight, it won't affect my driving." He laughed out loud. "Gottcha."

"How are you getting home?" Rayna wanted to be sure he wasn't driving.

"We've arranged for limousine service," Carrie said.

"The driver will be waiting for us right past Security." Evan looked around at the group of men and women waving placards at the arriving passengers. He turned his head toward Rayna. "Carrie said you're picking up a rental car at the airport."

"Yes, I've reserved one. Since it's so late, I'll call for a room before I pick up the car."

"Our offer's still open. You should stay with us," Carrie pleaded.

"We'd love to have you," Evan added with a grin.

"Well . . ." Rayna looked from Carrie to Evan, glanced at her watch and then said, "Maybe I should. How will we work it?"

"I'll give you our address and directions to the house. Let's exchange cell numbers, in case either of us has a problem."

Rayna headed toward Baggage while Evan continued to search for their driver.

After Rayna turned the corner, a middle-aged woman with short brown hair bumped into her. While they apologized to each other, the woman passed a package to Rayna, which she slipped into her overnight bag, and then hurried away.

Rayna was waiting for her suitcase to come up on the conveyor when her cell phone rang.

"It's Evan Mitchell, Rayna. I called the agency to find out where our chauffeur was. Turns out he was here early and left. Some damned woman told him we'd missed our flight. Now we'll have to wait an hour for another driver."

"Look, I can take you home," Rayna said. "The luggage from our flight still isn't up. Come to Baggage now and we'll go to the car rental together."

"Thanks, Rayna. You're a life-saver."

On the ride from the airport Carrie sat up front with Rayna, while Evan snoozed in the back seat. Carrie lamented about Evan's bad habits and how there was nothing she could do. Poor woman, Rayna thought, to have a double affliction—blindness and Evan Mitchell as a husband.

Rayna parked her car in the circular driveway of the Mitchell home, a sprawling Santa Fe in an upscale North Scottsdale neighborhood at the foot of the McDowell Mountains. She popped the trunk so Evan could get his luggage out. She took only her overnight bag.

As they stepped up to the front door, Evan remarked to Rayna, "I'm sure we've met before."

Rayna shook her head. "I don't think so."

"It'll come to me," he said.

He put his key in the lock and pushed the front door open. Rayna followed Carrie in. Evan dropped the suitcases in the entry hall and led the way across a marble floor into the living room. Rayna sat on the sofa, placing her overnight bag under the cocktail table in front of her. Carrie sat next to her.

"You have a beautiful home," Rayna said. "You must enjoy living here."

Evan nodded. "Best buy I ever made. It's doubled in value." He rubbed his hands together. "Let me get everyone a nightcap, then we'll show you around, Rayna. What'll it be? I'm having some Johnny Walker, but we've got everything."

"I'll have sparkling water."

"Don't you want something stronger?" Evan prodded. "It'll help you sleep."

"Water's good for me, thanks."

"Carrie, my dear, what'll you have?"

"Nothing for me."

Evan left the room to fetch the drinks.

Carrie stood. "I'm afraid I feel a headache coming on. I'm going to take something and go to bed." Rayna said good night, then Carrie headed for the stairs.

Rayna opened the zipper to her bag and adjusted the contents while waiting for Evan's return.

Within a couple of minutes he came back carrying a fifth of scotch and a shot glass for himself, and bottled water for Rayna. He handed her the water and sat down opposite her in an overstuffed chair. He poured himself a double. "To your health." He downed his drink while leering at Rayna.

When Rayna told him Carrie had gone to bed, his face lit up. She wondered if he were planning to come on to her.

"How about some nice music?"

She shook her head. "It'll disturb Carrie."

"Nah. Once her head touches the pillow, she's fast asleep. She'll be out until morning."

"I'd rather just talk." Rayna took a long swallow of her water and stared back at him.

He shook his head. "You know, you remind me so much of someone."

"From here or back in New Jersey?"

"Not from here. Probably, Jersey."

"You sure? Not many people look like me."

"You have any sisters? Maybe that's the connection."

She put her water bottle down and peered at Evan. "Actually. . ."

"You have photos?" He poured himself another drink and sunk back into his chair.

"I've got something better." She reached into her bag. She pulled out a revolver fitted with a silencer and pointed it at Evan.

He gasped and dropped his glass. "Are you crazy?"

She stood. "This is in memory of Maggie. Margaret Nevins. Remember her name, her car you wrecked, her mangled body?"

Rayna Nevins saw the spark of recognition in Evan Mitchell's frightened eyes. She fired the gun twice.

He opened his mouth, but fell over before he could get a word out.

"I guess you've figured it out."

She picked up her bag, slipped the gun and water bottle inside, and walked out the door.

EPHEMERA

Suzanne Flaig

I'm a pack rat. I pick up postcards, matchbooks, napkins, travel brochures—any souvenir freebies I can get my hands on. Anything with a logo, photo, advertisement or something to show where the item came from is fair game for my ever-growing collection. "Ephemera" is what the insiders call all paper collectibles.

When I got the chance to pick up a little extra cash working as a security guard at the annual Post Card and Ephemera Expo at the Phoenix Convention Center, I jumped at the offer. I hoped that during my breaks I could browse and chat with dealers from all over the country. Who knows? I might own something valuable.

The show didn't open to the public until Saturday, but the vendors started arriving Friday afternoon to set up their booths. Jimmy Weldon, a retired cop who does this security guard bit on a regular basis, got me the job. He knows I can use the extra money. In this case, with my passion for postcards, I would have paid them.

I used to be a cop, too, but I left the Phoenix PD a few years ago. I didn't quit because of the danger or the hours. You could say I had a slight problem with the male chauvinists who made up the bulk of the force. Short and blond, I look like a friendly poodle but can be as tenacious as a pit bull.

When the dealers began arriving with their collections and displays, I was on hand to help them unload and set up. It gave me the opportunity to get familiar with the people, their specialties, and how the booths were set up.

The first person I met on Friday afternoon was Joe Mackey, a local vendor who organized the show and was scheduled to do free appraisals. Jimmy took me over to meet him. His eyes did an appraisal of me, and I took an immediate dislike to the guy.

"She's a security guard?"

Jimmy grinned. "Don't judge a book by its cover, Joe."

Joe nodded at me, but his eyes burned with doubt. *Jerk*, I thought.

"Your job is to watch for shoplifters," Joe explained. "There are some rare vintage postcards out there worth thousands of dollars. If it's in mint condition and the artwork on the card is signed by a famous artist, like Rose O'Neill's kewpie doll series, you're talking big bucks."

Involuntarily, I sucked in my breath. I'd have to be sure to bring some of my postcards tomorrow and have them appraised.

Joe handed Jimmy two copies of the floor plan. "I have the first three tables by the front door, and this shows you the names and locations of all the other dealers. You know the routine. Get to know who's who today, so that when the crowd gets here tomorrow, you'll know where everyone belongs." His eyes were riveted on mine when he said, "I'm in charge here. Any problems, see me first."

Yeah, right, I thought. *Mr. Macho, the control freak.*

I was helping Leo and Peg, a couple from Milwaukee, set up their booth. They had arranged long boxes on the tables, so that the collectors could easily sort through their vintage postcards. As I bent over, picking a box up from the floor, I recognized the musky aroma of a high-priced cologne. He came up from behind.

"Hey Leo, who's your lovely assistant?"

I stood up to face the most gorgeous hunk I've ever laid eyes on. His dark brown eyes, the color of melted chocolate, sent shivers up my spine.

"Hi, Randy," Leo said. "Meet Lisa. She's one of our security guards for the weekend. Lisa, this is Randy Dayton from Tucson. He's got the booth next to ours."

"Let me take that for you," he said, reaching for the box. He leaned close and whispered a quiet warning in my ear, then stood up to place the box on the table.

"A security guard!" The man had a smile to die for. "You can guard me anytime. But you don't look too threatening." His once-over was much more pleasant than Joe Mackey's had been. This time it didn't bother me in the least.

"Whew! Is he charming, or what?" I whispered to Peg when he left.

"Yeah, as charming as the snake in the Garden of Eden," she replied, rolling her eyes. "Trust me. You don't want to get involved with that one."

Just then, Jimmy called from across the room, where he was standing with Mr. Nicholson, the manager of the Convention Center. "Lisa! C'mon over here a minute!"

Mr. Nicholson led us to the royal blue curtain that hung like a wall behind the last row of booths. "You need to keep an eye on this area." He pulled back on the curtain. "When a show doesn't use up the entire space, we partition off the unused area." He made it very clear he was the boss when he said, "Make sure nobody goes behind this curtain. I'm in charge here. Any problems, see me first."

Jeeze. Where did I hear that before?

"Yes sir," Jimmy said. "I've worked this show for the past two years, so I'm familiar with the procedure and the dealers. We won't have any problems."

"I hope not." Mr. Nicholson walked away.

Saturday went off without a hitch. I strolled up and down the aisles, watching for potential shoplifters. Collectors sat in chairs, comfortably sorting through the long display boxes of postcards. Shopping bags and purses were on the floor next to them. Unpaid-for merchandise could be easily slipped into the bags. My job was to catch shoplifters in the act.

I looked out over a sea of boxes filled with postcards from every place on the globe and about every subject imaginable. The view was dotted with islands of glass-enclosed treasures, racks of vintage sheet music, maps and travel brochures, and stacks of notebooks stuffed with matchbooks, bookplates, and trading cards. Shelves of antique books and magazines lined the walls.

I watched the dealers, too, occasionally stopping to chat or ask them questions about their specialties. The show featured quite a few postcard collectors, like Randy, Peg and Leo, but there were others selling a larger variety of ephemera.

Jeff and Mary Davis, a couple in their mid-thirties, had a huge collection of vintage sheet music. Mary got interested in it when her aunt gave her a box of music dating from the 1890s.

Another dealer, Donna Jensen, dealt strictly in animal ephemera: postcards, bookplates, greeting cards, posters, and other memorabilia with pictures of animals, especially cats, her favorite.

Then there was George Wilson who specialized in "automobiliana": advertising items from auto dealers and gasoline companies; travel maps; photos and postcards featuring automobiles; old Burma Shave highway signs.

There was something here for everybody.

During my lunch break, I took my small collection of postcards over to Joe Mackey for an appraisal.

He gave me a disdainful look when I handed over my grandmother's old album filled with postcards from all the places we'd visited on family trips since I was a little girl.

"I'm sure this has sentimental value," he said. "But this album is causing your postcards to deteriorate." He explained that I needed to invest in acid-free album pages if I wanted to preserve my collection. I promised that I'd transfer the rest of my postcards out of their shoeboxes as soon as possible.

Later that afternoon, I stopped to chat with Peg Lutz. "What did you mean yesterday when you told me not to get involved with Randy Dayton?" I asked.

"Oh, honey," she said, "that man fools around with half the women on the circuit. I don't know how he manages to keep track of them all. One of these days, he's gonna get into trouble either with a jealous girlfriend or some jealous husband. You mark my words."

"Jealousy can be deadly," I said through clenched teeth.

Just then, Randy walked over. "Word has it that you're a collector," he said. "Can I take a look at your stuff?"

"Joe already told me what my postcards are worth." I feigned indifference.

"You never know," he replied, flashing a dazzling smile that melted my resistance. "Different dealers are looking for different kinds of cards. Maybe you have something I can use."

Peg stood nearby, watching and listening. What did she think, I'd need a chaperone to protect me from the big bad wolf?

He leafed slowly through my postcards, studying the front and back of each one. I studied him, my heart tap dancing in my chest. A lock of his jet black hair fell forward over his handsome, tanned face, and he casually pushed it back in place. As I was fantasizing about running my fingers through his hair, he suddenly looked up.

"Sorry," he said, "you have some interesting cards, but nothing I can use right now. If you give me your address I'll put you on my mailing list—I distribute a little newsletter that you might be interested in."

I wrote my address down on the back of one of his cards, and returned to duty. But now I studied every female dealer, wondering if she were one of Randy's romantic "conquests."

Before I knew it, it was closing time.

"How do you like the job so far, Lisa?" Jimmy asked.

"It's great," I answered. "The only incident all day was when I interrupted Randy Dayton and Mary Davis, in what looked like a serious discussion behind Mr. Nicholson's dreaded blue curtain. They didn't seem too happy with me when I ran them out of there."

I wasn't too happy either, I thought. I didn't share that thought with Jimmy.

"I had to kick him out of there once, too, but he was with that lady who collects all the cat stuff."

I repressed the stab of jealousy that cut deeper than I wanted to admit.

Sunday morning started out with a bang. Before he even opened the doors to the public, Joe Mackey had to referee a shouting match between Jeff and Mary Davis. The air around booth twenty-five was definitely chilly the rest of the morning. Mary stood at one end of the booth, guarding her precious sheet music, her back turned on her husband.

Around ten, Donna Jensen caused a scene over at Randy's booth. She had her claws out, hissing at him like an angry cat. I settled her down and walked her back to her booth. Less than half an hour later, I passed Randy and Meredith Bell with their heads together in a back corner. Eyes red from crying, she kept insisting that he "reconsider."

To top it off, Jimmy and Joe Mackey had to break up an argument between Randy and George Wilson around eleven o'clock. Poor Randy. He was not having a good day.

Just when it had quieted down—the scream ripped through the crowd.

A collective gasp went up from the hall. Jimmy and I raced toward the end of the exhibit hall. Jimmy reached the hysterical woman first, and tried to calm her down.

I parted the blue curtain behind her, and stared at what had set her off. The big brown eyes of Randy Dayton stared back at me. The big, brown, *dead* eyes of Randy Dayton. He was lying face-up on the cement floor. It wasn't obvious at first what killed him, but it *was* obvious that he was stone, cold dead.

"Shit," Joe Mackey said, peering over my head. I closed the curtain before anyone else saw the body.

Curious onlookers surged forward. Jimmy took charge of the situation. "It's under control," he announced. "Nothing to worry about." They returned to their browsing.

To me, he whispered, "Don't touch anything or let anyone see this. I'll bring the cops in through the back." He escorted the hysterical woman to Mr. Nicholson's office, while I performed crowd control, keeping everyone away from the curtain and what was hidden behind it.

The police were there in less than ten minutes, but it seemed like it took forever. When they arrived and found the knife still stuck in Randy Dayton's back, they knew his death was no accident.

Jimmy muttered, "I signed on to look for shoplifters, not murderers."

The cops closed the Convention Center doors, and the Post Card and Ephemera Show officially ended. While the medical and forensic technicians did their thing at the crime scene, the homicide detectives questioned everyone.

A tall, powerful man with a blond crewcut and intense blue eyes headed our way. He had a chest that looked like it could stop bullets. I hoped he wasn't as tough as he looked.

"Hey, Jimmy, how are you?" He broke into a grin as they shook hands.

"Hi, Fred. I thought I retired to get away from you guys." He pointed to me. "Fred, Lisa."

Fred reached out a beefy hand. "Nice to meet you, Lisa."

"Likewise," I replied, comforted by his friendly manner.

"Why don't you fill me in on what happened here, Jimmy?"

"Well, Fred," Jimmy started, "it was pretty routine, quiet up until this lady poked her head behind the curtain at the end of the exhibit hall. Then all hell broke loose." He shook his head. "She saw the dead guy, and let out with a scream that could curl your hair. Luckily, we got to her quickly. Lisa took over crowd control and kept everybody away. I took the witness to Mr. Nicholson's office and called you."

"How many people saw the body?"

"We got there right away," he said. "The lady who found him, Lisa and I, and Joe Mackey were the only ones who looked behind the curtain. I told Mr. Nicholson."

Fred turned to me. "Do you have anything to add, Lisa?"

I took a deep breath. "I kept everyone away until you got here." I looked across the room, nearly empty now. "Nobody knew there was a dead body behind that curtain."

Nobody but the killer.

The atmosphere inside the Convention Center was like the prelude to a summer thunderstorm—hot, humid, heavy, oppressive, charged with electricity. The cops suspected everybody, and asked us all the same question: "When was the last time you saw the victim?"

Leo said he talked to Randy around eleven-thirty, when Randy had asked him to keep an eye on his stand so he could go out for lunch.

Randy's body was found just before noon.

I went over and sat next to Peg. She said, "I always knew Randy's fooling around would get him in trouble some day, but I never expected anything like this."

"You knew him pretty well, Peg. Do you have any idea who could have done this?"

"Take a number. A jealous husband. A jilted lover. One girlfriend who found out about another one. Who knows?"

"But you *might* know," I prodded. "Without even realizing it. Which of the women here was Randy involved with?" Peg was very observant. I was curious how much she knew.

"I know of three for sure: Mary Davis, Donna Jensen, and that new girl, Meredith Bell. But rumor has it that he had something going on this weekend with George Wilson's teenage daughter."

She was eager to share her gossip, and I encouraged her. "What can you tell me about them?"

"Mary Davis." Peg's face clouded over, and she hesitated. "Jeff could be nasty sometimes, but she wasn't about to leave him. I think she was just attracted to Randy because he was so sympathetic and attentive. She knew he wasn't serious, but she wasn't looking for a serious relationship, either."

"What about Jeff?" I asked. "How jealous was he? Could he have gotten angry enough to want to see Randy dead?"

"I don't know," she admitted. "They've had their share of fights, that's for sure."

"I know," I said. "Jeff and Mary were going at it this morning."

"No, I meant Jeff and Randy," she said.

"Oh. Well, what about the cat lady—Donna Jensen?"

"Don't let her sweet exterior fool you," Peg said. "She might like to collect postcards with cute little pictures of kitties and bunnies, but underneath she's a shark. She's probably the shrewdest businesswoman here. And the most unscrupulous. Collecting, for her, is not just a hobby. It's serious business. But her interest in Randy was purely physical."

"Sticking a knife in somebody's back is about as physical as you can get," I remarked. "Meredith Bell—I guess that was purely physical, too."

"Look at her," she said. "The sweet young thing. As far as Randy was concerned, it was just another fling. She expected more. I heard she's pregnant."

"What about the rumors about Randy and the Wilson girl? Doesn't she work as a waitress in the hotel restaurant?"

"Yeah, that's her. I saw them talking in the lobby last night, but any more than that is just gossip," she said. "Then again, knowing Randy…"

The body had been taken to the morgue, the hysterical woman was sent home, the crime scene investigators were back in the lab analyzing the evidence. The vendors were in their hotel rooms with the reminder not to leave town, and the custodian was scrubbing away the last vestiges of the crime scene in the convention center. Mr. Nicholson was in his office, probably knocking back a stiff one to calm his nerves. Fred, Jimmy and I were comparing notes in the hotel bar.

Fred had done background checks on all the vendors, and was shaking his head in disbelief.

"Motive, means, opportunity," he said. "Nobody can be eliminated."

"What do you mean?" Jimmy asked.

Fred stuck one beefy finger into the air. "Motive. The victim was a rat, both personally and professionally. He cheated Joe Mackey on a business deal, blackmailed Mary Davis, dumped Donna Jensen, and got Meredith Bell pregnant. On top of that, he entertained George Wilson's seventeen-year-old daughter in his hotel room last night." He shook his head. "That's just for starters."

A second finger shot up. "Means. The steak knife that killed him came from the hotel restaurant. Every one of the suspects ate in that restaurant last night and could have taken a knife. That proves premeditation."

"You're right," Jimmy said. "Lisa and I ate dinner there last night, too."

"What about opportunity?" he asked.

Fred sighed, and added a third finger, pounding his fist against the table. "Yeah. Opportunity. You tell me, Jimmy. Who was missing from the floor when the murder occurred? It was lunchtime. People were in and out. Half of the booths were empty or being watched over by the dealer in the next booth. First, one would run out for ten-fifteen minutes, then the other."

"That's right," I said. "Jimmy and I took lunch breaks between eleven and twelve, too. In fact, he had just come back when that woman found Randy's body."

"A single stab wound in the back, murder weapon left in the victim, no signs of a struggle. He must have been caught off guard," Jimmy said.

"Very little blood at the scene," I said.

"That's because the knife punctured the lung," Fred said. "Most of the bleeding was internal, into the lung. You could say the victim drowned in his own blood."

"What was the angle of the entrance wound?" Jimmy asked.

"Funny you should ask," said Fred. "Usually when someone is stabbed in the back, the attacker uses an overhand motion, and the entrance wound is downward. This one was thrust upward, as though the killer faced the victim and reached around to bring the knife up behind him."

"What's your theory, Lisa?" Fred asked.

I smiled. I wasn't used to the cops asking for my opinion, even when I was one of them. I let the scenario flow like a movie scene. "Let's say Randy had a rendezvous behind the curtain," I said. "It wouldn't be the first one this weekend, as Jimmy and I both witnessed. The woman, we'll call her the jilted lover, begs Randy to meet her as a desperate last attempt at reconciliation. She knows she'll be rejected again, but if she can't have him, nobody will. As they embrace, she drives the knife in to the hilt, using the element of surprise. Before he can even make a sound, he goes limp and she lays him down on his back and slips out from behind the curtain."

"I have trouble imagining that a woman would have the physical strength for this crime."

I gave him a look. "Do you think I'd have the strength, Fred?"

He smiled. "You're right, of course. I'm an equal opportunity cop. Everyone's a suspect. Your theory makes sense. But which woman? They all had a good reason to see him dead."

"Lisa caught Mary Davis arguing with Randy yesterday," Jimmy said. "She chased them out from behind the curtain."

"Witnesses told me Mary and Jeff Davis had a pretty serious argument this morning." Fred said. "Everybody heard it."

"I caught Randy behind the curtain with Donna Jensen yesterday, too," Jimmy said. "And then she had another run-in with him this morning. What about her?"

Fred nodded. "She admitted that Randy dumped her last night. But she's so tiny and feminine."

"She's about the same size as me, Fred," I admonished. "Don't let her looks fool you. Peg Lutz claims she's a barracuda."

"What about Meredith Bell?" Jimmy asked.

"Peg told me she's fairly new to the circuit," I said. "It didn't take Randy long to make a dishonest woman of her, did it?"

Fred said, "Actually, if you believe her story, he was dumping all the others to clear the way so they could get married…*if* you believe her story."

"Right," Jimmy said. "I guess that's why he had Wilson's seventeen-year-old daughter up to his room last night."

"She claims nothing happened," Fred declared. "She said she flirted with him at dinner and snuck up to his room later, uninvited. He sent her packing. She begged me not to tell her father."

"Maybe her father found out," Jimmy said. "Revenge on the man who sullied his daughter's reputation."

"This will be a tough one to solve," Fred admitted.

* * *

I didn't tell them about my rendezvous with Randy on Saturday night. Or that we had known each other before this weekend. I was more discreet than those other women. He promised me he would dump them all, for me. He lied. And he had to pay.

If I knew his address in Hell, I'd send him a postcard.

THE CALL FROM BEYOND

Reva Spiro Luxenberg

Sadie was a youthful seventy-four when Nathan, stricken with a heart attack, passed away in Maimonides Hospital in Brooklyn. Now, a year later, she comforted herself by sleeping on his side of their double bed. Sadie turned to her left side and snored lightly. Nathan's red plaid bathrobe that she wore to bed since his death fell open to reveal the black lace nightie he liked so much.

The telephone rang with a shrillness that shook her petite body. She moved her hand with the silver glitter polish artistically displayed on her nails to the phone on the night table. She picked up the receiver, too sleepy to say a word.

"Sadie, it's me. Nathan."

It sounded like Nathan's raspy voice, but it couldn't be. She had buried Nathan and his bones lay motionless in a grave in Washington Cemetery.

Sadie rubbed her eyes with her left fist. Some monster was playing a trick on her, calling her at 3 a.m., waking her up and telling her he was Nathan.

"Say something, Sadie. I ain't alive. Don't be scared *Bubbele*. I got permission to call you from the next world."

Sadie bolted upright, switched on the lamp, and rolled her tongue around. Her mouth was dry as cotton balls. She shivered as she drew Nathan's robe around her.

"Sadie! Believe me! It's your husband, Nathan. I ain't lying."

"Nathan? No. It's not Nathan. You're playing a trick on me. Nathan is dead and nobody calls from the next world. Stay on the phone while I record you and then I'll turn the tape over to the NYPD. They'll catch you."

"Sadie, you can't record my voice. The Lord doesn't allow no recording. Tell you what. I'll convince you." The voice paused. "Do you remember when Jeffrey was born?"

"Do I remember? How could I forget?"

"The first thing you said was, 'Nathan, I didn't give birth and it's not a boy.' Ain't that so?"

"Yes. But I told it to Jeffrey and he could've repeated what I said. So whoever you are who's calling me in the middle of the night could've heard it someplace."

"Okay, already. I'll tell you something that nobody knows but us. Do you remember what happened the first night we went on our honeymoon?"

Sadie's face turned borscht red even though no one was in the apartment. "Of course I remember. I never told a living soul I was so embarrassed."

"I was a real *shlemiel* when I looked at the checks people stuffed into my tuxedo pocket at the wedding, and I ignored you completely. You took your squirrel jacket and your evening bag and beat me over my stupid head."

Tears welled up in Sadie's faded blue topaz eyes. "Nathan, my love, my sweetheart, it is you!" Sadie sniffed, yanked a tissue from the pocket of the flannel robe, and blew her generous nose. "Why did you wait so long to contact me?"

"Do you think I spent a year in the next world doing nothing? I've been very busy. I had to go through every second of my whole life in front of a board of a thousand angels who weighed each deed before they presented their decision to the Lord who rendered His verdict. I wasn't sure what they'd do to me at the end, but I came through okay."

Sadie heaved a sigh. "I'm glad, Nathan. You were a wonderful man, a great husband, and a devoted father. I need your advice on something."

"My poor, poor wife. How can I help you?"

Grabbing the phone tightly, Sadie said, "Jeffrey is living with his wife in Chandler, Arizona and he wants me to move near him. I don't know what to do."

"So move. What's stopping you?"

"Oh," Sadie moaned. "I need to sleep in the same bed we always slept in and it's here in Brooklyn."

"Is that all? Sadie, take the bed when you move to Arizona."

"What a relief! I never thought of that. But tell me, Nathan, why is the good Lord letting you talk to me now? Is it my time to join you?"

"No. I ain't calling because of that. Sadie, hold on to your hat. I was murdered."

What?" Sadie screamed. "The doctor told me you had a heart attack. You were in the hospital, tubes coming out of you like you were a computer."

"I had a heart attack but I would've gotten better. It was Rudy. I never should've gone into partnership with him in the grocery. He was stealing me blind. When I found out, I carried on something awful and told the *gonef* I was going to tell on him and he'd spend years in the can. Then my ticker stopped ticking, and they took me to the hospital, but I was getting better."

"So how did he kill you, the lousy murdering . . . "

Nathan interrupted. "Don't say bad words, Sadie. Your every word is being noted by the angels."

"Okay. How did he do it?"

"He came at night after the nurse looked in on me. He stuck a needle full of his insulin into the back of my right knee. I had a convulsion, went into a coma, and died."

"*Oy vey!* I never liked that man, but I kept quiet because you took him in as a partner."

"Sadie, *Bubbele*, I have to get off the line. This is a long-distance call, very long distance, and it's costing a fortune. I love you. Don't worry about the next world. It's heavenly."

"Nathan, don't go. I love you. I miss you. Nathan? Nathan? I'll get the murderer. Don't worry. He'll suffer plenty."

Sadie couldn't wait until morning. She couldn't wait another second. She had to do something, but what? She padded into the tiny kitchen in her slippers and took out a bagel and cream cheese from the fridge. She toasted the bagel, spread on the cream cheese, and gobbled it down. The food cleared her head and an idea lit up her brain. She would call Rudy.

Picking up the receiver with a shaking hand, she dialed the murderer's number.

"Hello, Rudy? It's Sadie. I'm sorry to disturb you in the middle of the night, but I've been arrested and I'm at the 61st Precinct. Please bring me a coat and a thousand dollars for bail."

Rudy's voice was coated with sleep. "You've been arrested? Sadie Weinstein, arrested? For why are you arrested?"

"I'll tell you when you get here," Sadie said, shivering. She pulled her bathrobe closed.

Rudy spoke louder. "I haven't got a thousand."

Sadie spoke to the air. "Officer, will you take a check? Yes. You can bring a check, Rudy."

"I'll be there in an hour, Sadie. I need to shave and get dressed."

"Skip the shaving, Rudy. This is important. Just bring the check and the coat. And thank you."

After Sadie hung up she went to her closet and picked the first dress she saw. It wasn't her favorite, but time was of the essence. She had to get to the police station ahead of Rudy. She threw on her clothes, grabbed her pocketbook, took the elevator down to the main floor, and raced to her old Chevy Corsica parked in the street. She drove down deserted Coney Island Avenue, and pulled into a parking space in a dark street adjacent to the police station.

"I have to see a detective," she told the burly cop at the desk.

"What about, lady?"

"You wouldn't understand," Sadie said fisting her hands.

"If you want to see a detective, I have to know what it's all about."

The cop looked just like her second cousin, Morris, who she never liked because he was a complainer with a whining voice. For Nathan's sake she'd have to string him along. "I just got some important information about who murdered my husband, and if you don't let me see a detective I will tell my cousin, Muriel English, who is the top reporter for the *New York Times*. She'll write about this obstruction of justice and you'll be in hot water. No, not hot water. Boiling water."

"Okay, lady. You can see a detective. What's your name?"

"I'm Sadie Weinstein, widow of Nathan Weinstein."

Sadie waited on a bench for ten minutes that felt like ten hours. She twisted the handkerchief in her hand until it resembled a bagel. Finally a man with no hair and a toothpick in his mouth approached her.

"My name is Sadie Weinstein and I want to report the murder of my husband."

"I'm Detective Moskowitz," the bald man said as he removed one bent toothpick from the corner of his mouth and replaced it with another. "Follow me to my office."

In Detective Moskowitz's office, Sadie fidgeted with her fingers. "What's your husband's name and when was he murdered?" he asked as he began to scribble on a paper.

"Nathan Weinstein and he was killed last year. The man who murdered him is coming here very soon. He'll confess and then you can arrest him. But I have to make a phone call first to set it up. May I please use your phone?"

"Go right ahead. Just dial nine first." Detective Moskowitz picked up a folder on his desk and began reading a file in it, as Sadie called.

"Hello, Fanny. This is Sadie, here. Sorry to wake you, but it's important." Sadie held the phone away from her ear while her cousin ranted about being awakened at an ungodly hour.

"Fanny, I just found out that Nathan was murdered, and I need you to pretend to be a nurse who saw a fat man put a needle in Nathan's leg when he was in the hospital."

Detective Moskowitz looked up from his reading with an expression of wonder.

"Stop yelling," Sadie said, interrupting her cousin. "I know you don't lie, but sometimes it's necessary." She began to whisper, "Just remember, if it wasn't for me, you'd never have a date in your life. And if you want to meet another guy, I know one who'd be perfect for you."

Holding up his hand, Detective Moskowitz said, "Say goodbye."

"So long," Sadie said. "Just think about what I told you."

Detective Moskowitz gave Sadie an icy look. "I understand you're upset about your husband's death. Are you on medication? Have you been hospitalized for anxiety?"

"Are you crazy or something?" Sadie yelled. "I set a trap for this insect of a man and you are blocking this investigation."

"Mrs. Weinstein, why don't you go home and I'll take care of everything in the morning."

"I will not." Sadie leaned forward in her chair and glowered at the detective.

"Is this a closed case?" Detective Moskowitz asked.

"Not exactly," Sadie said biting down on her lip. "It was never reported as a murder."

"Why not?"

"I didn't know that my husband was murdered until an hour ago."

The detective picked up his pen, gnawed at it and grunted, "What happened an hour ago?"

Sadie squirmed in her chair. "My husband called me from the next world. I know it was my husband because he told me something that only the two of us knew."

Detective Moskowitz put his fingers in his ears and attempted to clear the passage. "Did you just say your dead husband called you?"

"I did and yes, he did. You're wasting time. The murderer is coming to this police station any minute and we should be in the lobby waiting for him to arrive." Sadie jumped up and moved to the door. Detective Moskowitz followed her.

"That's a good idea," he said looking relieved. "Let's go right now. Then if he doesn't show up, you can go home and I'll get back to my job."

"Oh, he'll show all right. Rudy may be a murderer, but he's always punctual."

Just as Sadie and the detective entered the outer lobby, a heavyset man in an overcoat with a black velvet collar rushed in carrying a woman's coat over his arm. He walked up to Sadie who looked at him like she could eat him up, grind up his bones, and spit them out.

Sadie, with a dramatic flair, pointed to his chest. "I accuse you of the murder of my husband."

The muscles in Rudy's face tightened. His close-set eyes fastened on the detective with the toothpick in his mouth. He laughed wildly. "Sadie, Nathan's death has affected your mind. You don't know what you're saying."

"I know about the syringe with the insulin."

Rudy's hands trembled. "Ridiculous. He died from a heart attack."

Sadie pointed her finger at him. "He was getting better. Your stealing gave him the heart attack. You didn't want him to tell on you so you killed him."

Rudy turned as white as the cheese in a blintz. "You can't prove a thing."

"I can," Sadie said. "I'll have his body dug up and forensics will find an overdose of insulin. You have diabetes. It would've been easy for you to kill him."

"Even if he died from insulin there is no proof that I did it," Rudy protested loudly.

Sadie smirked. "Proof? You want proof? I spoke to the nurse today and I convinced her to open up. She reluctantly admitted she saw you give Nathan a shot."

"The nurse saw me? No, she didn't."

Sadie moved closer to Rudy until she stood two inches from him. Raising her chin, her eyes like ice picks, she stared down the murderer until he stepped back and balled his fists.

Like a caterpillar, Sadie inched forward and pointed an accusing finger at Rudy. "She never reported it before because she told me she didn't have the time to get involved. She was in the midst of a nasty divorce and was afraid of losing custody of her children."

Rudy moved three feet back. "Sounds like you made up a soap opera."

Sadie sneered as she said, "Why don't we call her and find out the truth?"

"You're bluffing," Rudy protested.

"Okay, smart-aleck. I will call. May I use your phone, Detective?"

Detective Moskowitz shuffled his feet. "Sure. Why not?"

Fanny picked up the phone on the first ring. "Hello," she said calmly.

"Mrs. Robertson, this is Sadie Weinstein. I'm in the police station. I spoke to you before when you admitted you saw a man inject my husband with a needle the night that he died. I'm putting the suspect on the phone right now. All you have to say is, 'It's true,' and you won't be involved."

Sadie handed the phone to Rudy who clutched it like he was holding a dead chicken by its throat. "Hello, Mrs. Robertson. I was there that night, but it isn't true I put a needle in my partner's knee."

Sadie heard Fanny's cry. "It's true!"

"You see," Sadie said triumphantly as she faced the detective. "I never said he put the needle in Nathan's knee and Rudy implicated himself because the truth always comes out."

"All right, you win," Rudy said as he dropped the phone to the floor. "I did it, but Nathan deserved what he got. He was the cheapest man I ever knew, a skinflint of the first order."

"You're under arrest," Detective Moskowitz said as he spit out his toothpick and handcuffed Rudy. "You have the right to remain silent. You have the right to an attorney."

"I'm going home now," Sadie said with glee. "I'm expecting a long-distance call."

IDENTITY THEFT

Patricia Klemme

I don't know what happened to Edward. He was there and then he was gone. Now the police are looking for him, and I can't help them.

Edward was my neighbor and my former supervisor at work. A soft-spoken, slender, rather bland gentleman, he was competent at his work, a motivating supervisor, and apparently a skillful and prudent investor. He claimed successful investing ran in the family.

He announced his retirement at the age of forty-nine and introduced us to his replacement. At his retirement party, he confided he was glad he would still see me as a neighbor, although he expected to be traveling quite a bit.

Two days later he called me and said he had leased his house for one year to a woman named Gloria and he would be in Europe, Africa and Australia over the next year. Would I be willing to accept rent from this Gloria and deposit it to his local account? With some trepidation, I agreed to be a minimalist rental agent and wrote down his bank account information. I declined to accept responsibility for the care of his property or for finding another renter should this one decamp unexpectedly. Edward agreed in return to call me once a month to get an update of any potential problems and to verify the deposit. When I asked him to introduce me to Gloria, he chuckled lightly and invited me to walk over and introduce myself to her. He was already in New York, he said, and would be flying to London that night.

I had already seen the last of Edward, but as promised, he called to check on his property regularly, at least for the first four months.

Gloria proved to be the ideal tenant, paying her rent on time and caring for the house, lawn, and gardens as if they were her own. She hadn't been home when I went to introduce myself, so I left a note with my name and phone number plus directions to my house by way of the alley we shared. It was the beginning of tenancy by mail, she leaving her rent and newsy little notes clothes-pinned to my back door and I dropping off her receipt and a brief acknowledgment of her notes through the mail slot at her front door. She worked at night, she wrote, and slept in the daytime; she hoped one day we could meet. I didn't care whether we met or not so long as there were no problems.

But this—this putrefying body by my back fence—was a real problem.

After twenty-three years of hospital social work, I have a strong stomach for human effluvia emanating from the sick and wounded. But now, at four o'clock on a blistering August day in central Phoenix, I discovered this corpse with my nose before seeing it. I couldn't help but smell the beginnings of decay as soon as I came out the back door with the trash after work. I had steeled myself for finding a dead animal in the alley, but this body was human—a middle-aged, dowdily dressed woman whose face and limbs were already being attacked by birds and insects. Her short wavy blond-going-to-gray hair fell over the exposed side of her face, but I could tell she was no one that I knew. I called 911 and said I'd found a dead body in the alley. I was subjected to a series of ludicrous questions while the police were being dispatched.

Now the police were questioning me and the other neighbors under the direction of a detective sergeant from the Squaw Peak precinct, Sergeant Weldon. Weldon had nodded at me with a note of recognition on his face when he arrived. He kept glancing at me as if he were trying to place how he knew me.

Two years ago a burn unit patient at the hospital was under suspicion of arson for starting a fire at an abandoned business. Weldon had come in daily trying to interrogate the burn victim who was heavily sedated. We had gotten acquainted over that case, since I was the social worker assigned to the patient. Whether overly sedated or fearful of retaliation, the victim steadfastly refused to talk to Weldon. After a few days of this, I went in and asked him why he wouldn't talk to Weldon. The patient poured out his entire story to me. Then I was stuck, because it was privileged communication. It took me two more sessions to convince him to surrender and tell Weldon the whole story, a story that unlocked a whole string of arson-for-hire insurance scams. Weldon had been impressed and grateful. He invited me out to dinner at the time, but our schedules conflicted week after week and soon we lost contact. Even as I remembered, I saw recognition light up his face.

Nice to see you, too, I acknowledged silently as we watched the body being photographed by a crime scene technician. I had never seen the dead woman before, but I had a sinking feeling that it might be Gloria.

The uniforms were reporting back and, sure enough, there'd been no answer at Edward's house. Two other households had not responded to the police knocking. The one on the corner, I told them, was a Hispanic family. Although they were legal immigrants, they might be housing some undocumented aliens, cheap labor for their landscaping business. The family directly across the street from me was out of town somewhere in cool, comfortable Minnesota for the sweltering months of Phoenix's summer. A pet sitter came by every morning to care for their two cats and the houseplants, and a neighborhood teen was mowing their lawn periodically.

That left the elusive Gloria, who was probably reposing at our feet. And Edward, who was God knows where. Sergeant Weldon seemed fixated on my absent neighbor, even though I assured him Edward hadn't been in Phoenix for over a year.

Weldon directed one patrol officer to verify the vacationing family's absence with other neighbors and sent me with a Spanish-speaking officer to persuade the Gonzales family to answer a few questions. Officer Beltran and I were able to get Mr. Gonzales to open the door. Beltran exuded Latin charm and rapid-fire Spanish. Soon Jorge was smiling and nodding and inviting us in. Beltran dismissed me from further duty and directed me to advise Sergeant Weldon that he would do preliminary interviews, but it was going to take some time.

In my absence, the crime scene folks had made substantial progress. I knew that, because the mortuary attendant was zipping up a vinyl body bag as I rounded the corner to the back of my fence. The stench of decay continued to permeate the air in the alley and I muffled my nose and mouth protectively. I reported to Weldon that the Gonzaleses were indeed harboring smuggled, undocumented aliens: about thirty of them. He rolled his eyes but was no more surprised than I was. Illegal aliens are an on-going fact of life in Arizona. In exchange for cooperating as potential witnesses, the police would look the other way and refrain from reporting them to Immigration.

The medical examiner's van and two Phoenix police cars raised dust in the alley as they departed. I asked Weldon to let me take a break. He agreed but exacted my promise to return within thirty minutes. I took my garbage bag, which I had abandoned at the gate when I first saw the body, and deposited it into the dumpster. A uniform promptly made me remove it and lectured me about contaminating evidence. I plucked it out and handed it to him. He started to give it back to me, but I reminded him it now had 'evidence' on it; I couldn't possibly be responsible for evidence. I smiled grimly and stalked off.

Inside, I washed my hands and face, combed my hair and—for good measure—brushed my teeth. I changed out of my summer, linen-blend suit and low heels into jeans, a t-shirt and walking shoes. I loved that work outfit, but now I wanted to burn it. I compromised by bagging it to go to the dry cleaners and putting it on the front porch. Even though I had tightly knotted the bag, I thought I could still smell the stench.

I returned to the alley. Suddenly I felt exhausted. I must have looked funny, because Weldon asked if I was okay. Yeah. Just another day in the neighborhood I thought: a dead body in my alley, thirty or so UDA's in my neighbor's house, a missing tenant who might well be the deceased, and Weldon looking at me impatiently. I snapped to, realizing he had asked me another question. He gestured toward my back door, and I got it. Sure, come in, I invited.

Seated at the kitchen table, Weldon began to interrogate me about Gloria and Edward. I set out some cookies and put on a pot of coffee. Edward Kerodos, formerly a supervisor for a hospital social services office, had leased his home to Gloria Martinez, a spinster in her fifties who kept pretty much to herself. A white Taurus sedan registered in her name was parked in the driveway, but there was no answer to the doorbell or knocking. Weldon had authorized a wellness check, a procedure followed when someone may be ill or injured and unable to respond. There was no sign of Gloria or Edward or anyone else inside. A purse with identification, keys, and all the items of a woman's handbag indicated that Gloria hadn't just run out to the grocery store or to work. The picture on Gloria's driver's license wasn't too good. Although it was dated within the past year and had Edward's address on it, the plastic was worn and a glint of light reflected in Gloria's glasses made the image ineffective for positive identification. Likewise, the body hadn't been easy to look at. Birds had already pecked out the eyes and insect larvae were deposited in every moist orifice. Weldon said she had been out there as much as a day or two. The Arizona heat accelerates decomposition in every way. Weldon and the medical examiner believed she had been strangled in her home but abandoned before she died. They theorized that she had regained consciousness and tried to call for help. Both phones had been ripped out and the likely places for valuables, such as dressers and the china cabinet, had been ransacked. She had evidently tried to come to my house for help, but died from heart failure or asphyxiation en route.

Weldon wanted me to go over with him and see if I could identify anything missing. I reminded him that Edward and I had had a cordial, over-the-back-fence relationship. In the twenty-some years I'd known him and Rick, I'd never set foot in that house. Rick? Who was Rick, Weldon wanted to know.

Rick. Rick was Edward's nephew, a handsome young man who had lived with Edward since Rick's teens. He made himself useful by caring for Edward's lawn and gardens. Rick worked part time jobs for pocket money and seemed content to mooch off Edward's largesse until about two years ago when Rick moved away. Weldon was adding notes to his flip-pad as I talked. Since Rick left, Edward had mowed his own lawn and hired Jorge to trim the oleanders and maintain the flowerbeds. No, I didn't know where Rick moved. I was becoming irritated with Weldon's persistent questioning. I don't have to know my neighbors well. I knew them well enough to know they were easy-going, pleasant people who wouldn't hurt a fly. I took the cookies away from Weldon and got up to make a couple of sandwiches. As disgusting as the day had been, I still felt hungry.

Weldon answered his cell phone when it sounded off with the theme from *Shaft*. While listening to the caller, he munched on the ham and cheese sandwich I gave him. He stopped mid-chew and glanced over at me. Swallowing, he acknowledged his caller's last statement and slapped the phone closed. Out the back door we went and quickly marched across the alley, I with my sandwich in hand and he calling directions to the uniform guarding the entrance to Edward's place. The uniform let us into Edward's kitchen door. Weldon put on a pair of latex gloves and handed a pair to me, reminding me that even with the gloves on, I was not to handle anything.

A technician was dusting a glass-fronted buffet for fingerprints. Weldon went to a desk in the living room and began looking at every paper and piece of mail on it. I wandered through the dining room and living room looking but not touching. I looked at photographs of Rick on the mantelpiece. I thought it odd that Edward had left them, and that Gloria hadn't moved them or put them away.

I ventured down the hall looking in the bedrooms and bathroom. The master bedroom had been trashed. Paintings had been thrown into a corner, the bedding and mattress were askew on the bed frame, clothing and shoeboxes littered the floor, and dresser drawers were left open with disheveled contents. A large jewelry box had been emptied, and there was no sign of other valuables. In the master bathroom, the medicine cabinet was open, and three prescription bottles labeled for Gloria Martinez lay empty in the sink. I identified one of the medications as a common hormone replacement for menopausal women. The other two I didn't recognize.

I moved on to the other bedroom which appeared to be completely undisturbed. The bed was made, belongings were put away neatly on shelves, and Central High School memorabilia graced the walls. This was Rick's room, left looking the way he must have left it two years ago. I yawned involuntarily and looked at my watch. Only eight-thirty, I marveled. It seemed like days had passed since I got home from work.

A commotion at the front of the house got my attention. Two of the uniforms were taking down a tanned, dark-haired man and handcuffing him. I moved closer as Weldon motioned for the cop to turn the intruder over. Rick! I must have said it out loud because Rick looked up from the floor and glared at me. The officer holding him down extracted Rick's wallet and pulled out a driver's license, handing it to Weldon. Weldon read the name Richard Martinez out loud. Rick turned his gaze to Weldon, but didn't answer. Weldon signaled the uniform to release him and assured Rick he'd be trussed up again like a Thanksgiving turkey if he failed to cooperate. Rick still looked surly, but nodded.

In short order, Weldon elicited several items of information. No, Rick was not related to Gloria Martinez. He claimed the last name was just a coincidence. No, he didn't know Gloria Martinez and had no idea who she was. Yes, he was Edward Kerodos's nephew, but he had been in Mexico the past two years working in a Pemex oil field. I had trouble believing that one; Rick was not famous for hard work, but maybe he had matured. Certainly, his swarthy tan gave credence to outdoor living. No, he had no idea where his uncle was. He didn't even know Uncle Edward wasn't living here. Rick squirmed slightly as Weldon asked about his contacts with his uncle. He finally admitted his uncle had thrown him out on his twenty-fifth birthday, but hey, it wasn't his fault his uncle was a miserly bastard with no sense of family loyalty. Rick's only means of retaliation was to shut his uncle out of his life. Rick had come home now to prove to his uncle that he had grown up and was earning his own keep. He even had savings stored up to boot. I watched Weldon's face as if it were the tracer arm on a lie detector's graph. He wasn't buying it either. He glanced over at me. He turned back to Rick and asked him how many times he'd been in the house this week. None, Rick asserted. Not at all in the last two years? Not at all. Not even once in the last week? No, Rick insisted.

Weldon called the chunky fingerprint tech over and told him to get Rick's fingerprints. Rick started to object, and then subsided when Weldon pointed out it shouldn't be a problem if Rick hadn't been here for two years. I watched Rick's face as the technician rolled one finger pad after another over the ink and the file card. He wasn't exactly sullen, but he wasn't pleased either. Weldon told Rick to stay put until we returned and signaled the uniform to keep an eye on him.

Weldon motioned me to follow him and off we jogged to Jorge's house to follow up with Officer Beltran. Beltran was in the living room finishing an interview with the last three of the undocumented aliens. His report came as no surprise. No one had seen or heard anything. Most were in transit from one place to another and had not been outside of the house since they were smuggled in. Members of Jorge's family denied knowing the woman renting Edward Kerodos's house. Even their young son, Julio, had only seen her from a distance. Julio, fluent in English compared to his parents, had never talked to her. When pressed for a description, he said she was old. Julio and I had quite different opinions about her age, but I chalked it up to a child's perception of old versus the perspective of middle age. Then I remembered. We didn't even know if the deceased *was* Gloria Martinez.

The theme from *Shaft* sounded off again and Weldon took his cell phone into the hallway, although there was no way to get away from people anywhere in this unofficial hostel. To my dismay, he told me we were picking up Rick and going to the morgue at the invitation of the medical examiner. I protested that neither Rick nor I could help since neither of us knew Gloria Martinez by sight. Weldon didn't care. We were the likeliest to have some subconscious bit of information that might be jarred loose by further interrogation. Ah. I was a suspect, too, I suddenly realized. It was not a happy thought.

Weldon started in on Rick as soon as he was brought to the car. Rick answered his questions at first but then dug his heels in. Rick had not been in touch with his uncle at all for two years and had no idea where Edward was or even if Edward were alive. I wondered about that myself. Edward hadn't called or contacted me in any way after the fourth month of his trip. I had gone on depositing the rent checks and the bank had cheerfully accepted them. Since Gloria hadn't reported any problems and was taking good care of the place, I hadn't given any thought to Edward's silence over the past few months. I volunteered that information to Weldon. We rode in silence to the county morgue after that.

The medical examiner's offices smelled stuffy and antiseptic. The air conditioner fan was blowing, but the air was stifling, as if the compressor were failing. Rick didn't want to be here. Inside the entrance he told Weldon he was leaving, that Weldon had no right to hold him. Weldon smiled grimly and spun Rick into a chokehold. He whispered briefly into Rick's ear and released him. Rick followed obediently without further protest. Weldon pressed a square panel next to double doors, which sighed open automatically onto a broad, white hallway. A buzzer sounded in the distance and a man in green hospital scrubs came out to meet us. Weldon parked us in an airless meeting room and closed us in while he went to talk with "Dr. Death." I thought about making conversation with Rick, but he had that sullen look about him again. I pulled my chair up to the table and wearily rested my forehead on my crossed arms. I peeked every so often, and I realized that I didn't trust Rick. By the look on his face, he didn't trust me either. We both jumped when the door opened.

Weldon introduced "Dr. Death" whose real name was Dr. Carmichael. He joined us at the table and told us more than I wanted to know about the death of the presumptive Gloria Martinez. She had indeed had a prolonged and miserable death. Sergeant Weldon watched us both closely as Dr. Carmichael continued to describe Gloria's last hours. He took pains to tell us that Gloria had fought back and that the killer's skin tissue had been recovered from Gloria's fingernails and teeth. This would be valid DNA matching evidence in court. Then Carmichael led us into a family viewing room to see the deceased. He asserted we would both be able to help with identification. I looked at Weldon who was watching us both intently. I started to explain to Dr. Carmichael that neither of us had met Gloria. Rick was backing away in spite of Weldon's scrutiny, but Weldon grabbed his arm tightly. Carmichael pulled the sheet down and Rick made a strangled sound. Carmichael had combed back the corpse's hair and dressed it in a man's white shirt and necktie.

Edward! This was unmistakably Edward Kerodos. I said so. Rick was trying to wrench himself from Weldon's grasp. I backed into a corner as Weldon fought to subdue Rick Martinez. A morgue security guard charged in and helped Weldon get Rick handcuffed. Rick quit struggling and allowed himself to be pushed into a chair while the guard stood over him.

Carmichael explained to us what he'd already told Weldon by phone. In the autopsy the deceased was identified as a male-to-female transgender with completed surgical reassignment, probably done in Europe by the looks of the surgical details.

"Rick," I asked, "what do you know about this?"

He shook his head from side to side angrily. "I didn't kill him. I just came back to get him to release my inheritance from the trust. I don't want to wait until I'm thirty. I don't even know who this woman is!"

"You do know. It's your uncle, Rick. What did you think when you saw her? Did you realize it was your uncle?"

He dropped his chin to his chest and let loose a low anguished whine. Tears formed at the corners of his eyes. "He looks just like my mother," Rick whispered. "My mother's been dead since I was twelve. When I opened the door and saw her...When I saw him looking just like her... He shouldn't have done that. He shouldn't have made himself look just like her." He gave himself over to the tears.

"What was your mother's name?"

"Gloria. He even took her name." Rick's voice shook with anger and grief. "I didn't mean to kill him. I was just so angry."

"And why did you ransack the house?" I asked gently. Weldon was watching and making notes but not interfering.

"I wanted..." he began tentatively. "I wanted to find anything he had of my mother's. I wanted to get my trust papers so I could get my inheritance. My mother left her jewelry and a $50,000 trust fund for me. He had it all."

"You were afraid he wouldn't give it to you? So you killed him to be sure you'd get your inheritance?"

"No. I killed him for trying to become her. For making himself just like her. No man should do that to himself, but he had to look just like her and take her name. He just took over her life as if she never existed. She was my mother. She didn't deserve to have him steal her life."

THE LAST HABANO

Howard B. Carron

The first thing you notice upon entering the room is the complex aroma of fine cigars: a medley of toasted nut laced with a waft of Dutch chocolate, French Roast coffee, and cedar in the background compounded by the warmth of the leather chairs grouped around the room. The cigars held by the guests enjoying a quiet moment represent Dominican, Nicaraguan, Honduran, Ecuadorian cigars wrapped mostly in Connecticut Shade. Here and there a full-bodied double corona maduro makes its presence known. The warm walnut panels are complemented by the discreetly lit hunting prints on the wall. The wait staff, dressed simply in black trousers, white shirts, and black bow ties, circulate quietly and efficiently delivering the beverages of choice.

I spotted my amigos, a group of reporters and writers, who share my appreciation of fine cigars, whiskies, and other libations. Our conversations often explored the recent news of the day or comedians we loved from the past. Some of us tend to be rather long in the tooth. We began discussing one of our long-standing subjects: Cuban cigars. We were exploring the pros and cons of particular tobaccos, whose seed had been smuggled and transplanted from Cuba to the Dominican Republic, Nicaragua and Honduras, and whether they were as good as we believed the original to be. As usual, we ended up sharing anecdotes pertaining to cigars. Someone said to me, "Enrico, it's your turn."

After a few moments of thought, I removed a worn, softly faded news clipping from my wallet. The article from The *Arizona Sentinel* discussed the strange deaths of Emilio Santiago and his father-in-law, Jorge Valenzuela. The coroner's office reported that murder and suicide were indicated and that police were investigating. After the article made the rounds, I carefully replaced it in my wallet and began.

When I was growing up in Dade County, Florida, I often made trips to visit friends and relatives in Ybor City, which is where I met Jorge. He worked in a little shop as a *torcedor*, a master cigar roller, making 150 perfectos a day. Hand-made cigars are constructed in three parts—filler, binder and wrapper. I loved to watch him deftly grasp a handful of tobacco, place it just so in his hand and quickly roll it into a tube. Grasping his *chaveta*, a traditional flat bladed knife, he quickly trimmed the excess tobacco. Next came the binder, carefully trimmed by two rolling cuts and then placed into the wooden forms stacked in front of him. After 45 minutes the tobacco was fully formed. Choosing a special leaf of Connecticut shade wrapper, he trimmed it by removing the central vein making two pieces, and he was ready to roll a perfecto. Jorge had started his apprenticeship as a youngster in Cuba and came to Florida after the "trouble" as he always put it. Only a master *torcedor* could do justice to this shape. Gently he laid out the wrapper and quickly applied some vegetal glue to the edge, rolling it on a 45-degree angle, quickly finished the cigar, ending with a few expert twists on each end.

He would then look up at me and smile and ask if I would like to try my hand at his craft. It wasn't until I had known him for five years that I took him up on this challenge. We became friends, and when I was at college, about once a month he would send me a beautifully wrapped cigar. After I graduated from Journalism school and was working for a local publication, I would visit with him. One day, he invited me to his home for coffee and a cigar.

As I spoke, I could feel the smoking room receding, and I was back outside Jorge's house.

I arrived, rather curious at what I would find, and was pleasantly surprised when a young lady opened the door. She introduced herself as Lilia, Jorge's daughter. I knew Jorge had a daughter but I had never seen a picture of her. And what a picture she was: long, shimmering, black hair; perfectly formed eyebrows over luminous oval shaped black eyes; a perfectly shaped nose and full red lips. She had the kind of smile that tightened a band across my chest, and I was almost incoherent as I introduced myself, totally captivated and instantly smitten. She laughed, a sound that would put a crystal bell to shame, and led me into the *sala*. The living room walls were covered with memorabilia from Cuba: framed cigar box labels, wood forms for pressing cigars and an old-fashioned cigar cutter on a wooden base. The furniture in the room was worn but not shabby, just comfortably lived in. There was an aroma of lemon oil polish intermingled with the rich memory of tobacco. Lilia led me to a comfortable rattan chair and said, "Papa is grinding the coffee beans, and he will be right out." She left the room leaving a tantalizing scent of her presence, a tropical breeze alive with citrus and a wisp of frangipani blossoms. A few moments later, Jorge appeared with two cups and saucers and a steaming carafe of coffee. The fresh aroma was incredibly enticing, and Jorge nodded approvingly at my sniffing and smiling.

He said, "When I first came to the *Los Estados Unidos*, I couldn't understand why Americans were satisfied with instant coffee. It was difficult for me to find a place that made decent espresso except in a Cuban restaurant. Now, *gracias a Dios*, they have discovered not only good coffee and brandy but also good cigars as well."

We chatted about my job, the resurgence of the cigar industry, and all about the old days before and after Castro. I found out that Lilia was his only child and that his wife had passed on when Lilia was only six, fourteen years previously. At that moment, Lilia appeared at the door obviously dressed to go out. She wore a pair of dark colored jeans beautifully cut to emphasize her decidedly attractive figure, with a gold link belt, one end hanging down her right side. A cream colored long-sleeved blouse accentuated her breasts without being déclassé; a rust colored scarf with flashes of gold threads around her throat complimented both her skin and the pair of small gold hoop earrings encircling a sparkling small diamond. Black pumps with a discreet heel completed the ensemble. Even without trying she projected a sense of identity and strength with an underlying foreshadowing of vulnerability. Her beauty left me breathless. She turned towards Jorge and told him, "Papa, I am meeting Emilio for dinner. I left your dinner in the microwave, just set it at reheat and it will be ready in a few minutes." She seemed to float over to Jorge. She gave him a kiss on the cheek, flashed me a smile, and was gone.

"*Madre de Dios*," Jorge said, "*No le gusto, Emilio*, but Lilia thinks he is wonderful. What is a father to do?"

Suppressing my disappointment at this information I arched my eyebrows questioningly. After a moment's consideration, Jorge continued. "Emilio is very handsome, likes the good life, and is willing to do anything to keep himself in that lifestyle. He is a talented musician but can't keep a job because he is so impatient. He is now studying to be a real estate broker, and I hope he will settle down. He and Lilia are planning to be married next month and move to the southwest. Next year I will retire and perhaps join them."

Jorge sighed and then, as if remembering he had company, turned and told me that he had a real treat in store for me. He opened a beautiful humidor beside him and took out a Churchill cigar without a label. He looked at it with such delight that my curiosity was heightened.

"One of my nephews brought this with him from Cuba about five years ago and I have a few left. This is a Romeo y Julieta, and it is my favorite. I want you to join me in enjoying these cigars."

Now, I had smoked Cuban cigars before but had never had a R & J. After admiring the rich, oily dark wrapper and inhaling the warm aroma we clipped, toasted and lit our cigars sitting back in companionable silence, enjoying the afternoon.

Shortly after that visit, I was transferred to Phoenix. In the crush of learning my new job at a regional magazine, I pushed Jorge and Lilia to the back of my mind. So I was pleasantly surprised to look up from my desk one morning to find Jorge standing there, white suit, plantation Panama, and a big smile. Since we had so much to talk about, we drove to a "cigar friendly" restaurant on Camelback Road and talked and smoked for over an hour.

Jorge was quite animated about his new home in Paradise Valley. I raised my eyebrows at this posh location. Recognizing my inquisitive look, he explained, "Emilio is now a very successful broker and has a beautiful home with so many rooms that I can get lost. Lilia is caught up in the swirl of society, and we have many parties at the house. I have my own two rooms, and we have a maid and a cook."

All of this was said in one breath as if saying it quickly could cover his discomfort. Sensing my next question he hurried on to explain. "Enrico, I do not wish to burden you with my troubles but, despite the difference in our ages, you have always been a good listener. I am sure that Emilio is involved in something that is not good. I hear him and Lilia arguing all the time."

I realized that Jorge, normally reticent, must have had some serious concerns or he would not be airing family problems to an outsider. "Well, Jorge," I said, "some marriages are a little rocky occasionally," although I had no experience on which to base my opinion.

"Sometimes I hear the arguments and they are mostly about his womanizing and shady friends. Lilia will not discuss this with me, but I was wondering if perhaps you might look into what he is doing through some of your reporter friends."

Ted L'Orange worked the police beat and was privy to the more sordid side of our community. I asked him what he had heard about current activity in the drug trade and if Emilio's activities were part of any ongoing investigation. He gave me the information I needed. All bad. Emilio was suspected of laundering Colombian drug money through his real estate deals and a number of complicated company maneuvers. He also had a serious reputation of philandering.

A week later I met with Jorge again, and when I related the information, his reaction was one more of resignation than of surprise. We smoked our cigars very quietly in an almost restrained manner and then he left.

Two weeks later I received a phone call from Jorge.

"Enrico, I am calling to say goodbye. I am going on a journey." And that was it!

Shortly after our conversation there was an item on page four of the *Arizona Sentinel*, the one I showed you.

Two days after the article appeared, Lilia showed up at my office, looking wan and strained but lovely nevertheless. I didn't know if she knew of my involvement, and I wasn't going to tell her. There was a long pause before she started to speak.

"Enrico, you were always a good friend and listener to Papa, and I hope that you will be my friend also. We have no family out here and all of Emilio's friends have disappeared suddenly. I need to tell someone about what happened to Papa and Emilio."

This was her story.

"A month back," she continued, "Papa had a serious argument with Emilio about his business dealings and his treatment of me. Emilio called Papa a relic from the past who was only good for rolling cigars. I tried to straighten things out between them but neither of them would listen to me. That evening Emilio came home quite drunk and slapped me. This was not the first time. Then he told me that I was a serious burden to his life and that there were plenty of pretty girls out there who didn't have interfering old men around spying on everything. Our bedroom door was slightly ajar, and I saw Papa standing in the hallway.

"The next day Papa asked Emilio to meet with him and see if they could patch things up between them. At about 3:30 in the afternoon Emilio came home and Papa, dressed in his white suit and Panama hat, went into the *sala*. I sat on the veranda behind the partially closed shutters, out of sight, and watched. I heard Papa say to Emilio, 'I must honestly say I have not been happy about the way that you have treated my Lilia. Perhaps we can smoke a cigar and have some brandy and see what we can do about this.'

"With the arrogance of someone who has made up his mind already, Emilio nodded and sat down.

"'This is a truly fine cognac, Remy Martin Extra Fine Champagne Cognac,' Papa said, as he poured the cognac into the snifters. 'Sense the aroma, hold it up to the light and see its color, swirl it in the glass to see the "legs." Can you smell the flowers, the dried apricots, and the vanilla?'

"Emilio didn't answer. With one gulp, he downed the liquid, baring his teeth in a grimace as the fiery ambrosia coursed hotly towards his stomach. Papa shook his head.

"'No, no Emilio, you must sip a fine cognac, just the tip of your tongue and savor the wonderful flavor. Can you taste the pears, plums, walnuts, honey, and spice? It flows down like a velvet glove caressing the throat. Here, try it again.'

"While Emilio held the glass, Papa clipped, toasted, and lit one of his favorite Romeo y Julieta Cuban cigars, smiling complacently. Emilio raised his voice, looked at Papa, and in a hard voice said, 'This is nonsense, and you know it old man. Lilia may be your daughter, but she is my wife. Not for long,

I may add. I'll treat her any damn way I want and there is nothing you can do about it.'

"Papa lifted the decanter and filled Emilio's glass again saying, 'Have some more cognac, Emilio. Perhaps we can find a way to solve this problem.'

"Emilio tossed back the cognac once again and Papa shook his head in disappointment. Suddenly, a look of fear came across Emilio's face as he struggled to rise to his feet. His eyes widened, first with astonishment and then with the realization that he was dying. As his sensory motors shut down, his mouth flapped like a fish out of water. Then his body relaxed. The glass fell from his hand, and his head tipped back with his arms splayed outwardly.

"Papa sat quietly and puffed on his cigar and then called to me on the veranda. 'Come in Lilia, all is well again, but I want to see you once more.'

"I stumbled into the room and hugged Papa. As he stroked my hair slower and ever more slowly, I realized that he too would soon be gone. I looked up at him. He smiled at me and said, '*Que lastima*, I will miss you, my little one.' He put the cigar in the ashtray, closed his eyes and was gone.

"Enrico, what will I do now?"

I held Lilia, who, by this time was crying gently into my chest, and I, too, stroked her head, wondering what lay ahead for her.

The next day, in the morning mail, I received a letter from Jorge and a cigar, a Romeo y Julieta, wrapped carefully within a plastic bag with a damp tissue to keep it from drying out. There was a little note of explanation:

Enrico, I have removed Emilio from my Lilia's life and since the doctor has told me that I will be dead in three weeks from prostate cancer, I have decided that this is the only honorable way. I have seen in your eyes that you care for Lilia, and I hope that you can help her out. Enjoy my last Habano. Vaya con Dios, Jorge

Everyone was quiet at the table and then we nervously began looking at watches; some of us scurried to pay the bills.

"Until next time," I said as I rose from the chair. "My wife is picking me up shortly."

We all moved towards the front door. As I stepped out into the street I heard someone in the group ask, "Whatever happened to Lilia?"

There was laughter.

Then came a response.

"Take a look at the beautiful black-haired woman who's picking Enrico up. And you'll know."

STELLA

Deborah J Ledford

The call woke me at two a.m. Disoriented, receiver bobbing in my sleepy hand, I heard the frantic, faraway voice of my fifteen-year-old on the other end.

"Mama?"

"Stella?"

"Mama, come get me."

Twenty minutes later I found myself in the parking lot of a run-down Eloy hotel I drove past every weekday on my way to the Cash 'n Carry, where I stood all day. Swipe. Beep. Swipe. Beep. Fake smile. "Have a nice day." After four years, I saw inventory in my dreams. Only three more hours until I'd have to start all over again.

Teeth clenched, I was beyond angry. I replayed the words of warning I had spoken just the night before.

"Stella, this is it. No more sneaking out. No more next time."

But here I was, shivering and annoyed, walking toward the "next time."

The squeal of tires rounding the bend alerted me to a battered pickup bouncing through the lot, coming right for me. I took cover behind my beat-up Hyundai as the pickup passed the empty parking space beside me and skidded to a stop in a cloud of white smoke and burning rubber. The driver backed into the spot and jumped from the truck, slamming the rusting door after him.

Curious, I watched as the angry driver burst through the double doors of the hotel and disappeared inside. When I walked past the ancient, massive truck I noticed a small figurine on the dashboard. A plastic horse stood on its back legs, reared back, front feet kicking out. I could almost hear it whinny.

Squinting in the bright, shabby lobby, I searched for the elevator. The man stood in front of it staring up at the numbers. While we waited, I studied him. Arms crossed over a substantial chest, cuffs of a denim shirt unsnapped. Blond hairs curlicued from under a brushed silver watchband. Weathered fingers impatiently tapped his elbows. No wedding ring. My mood brightened. I wished I'd taken the time to apply lipstick.

Finally, the doors opened. We entered and faced them again. Slightly behind the man, I watched him in the reflection of the distorted mirrors of the doors. A rodeo belt buckle the size of a dessert plate caught my eye. The tapered waist. My head dropped lower. How long since I'd been with a man? Three years? Four? Blushing, I urged my attention back to the lit panel. We were headed for the same floor.

A ping filled the tiny compartment announcing our arrival. He shot out as the doors opened. Standing in front of a placard on the wall showing how the room numbers ran, we both stared from it to crumpled notes in each of our hands. He turned left, I went right. Scanning numbers on the passing doors, I stopped. Shaking my head, I turned around and hurried back the way I had come.

When I found room 408, I was surprised to see him standing in front of it.

He pummeled the door four, five, six times.

"Frankie! You in there? Open up the door!" His booming voice shook in anger.

Silence.

He mumbled something.

I shuffled one foot to the other and he noticed me for the first time. "You got one in here too?"

I nodded.

"Been lookin' all night."

"I'm sure there's nothing to be worried about."

"You don't know my Frankie." He pounded again. "Open up the damned door!"

I felt anxious for the first time since Stella's call. She was constantly giving me hardship, but she had never gotten into any real trouble. My heart skipped, fearing she was in there with the boy named Frankie. I joined him in the pounding.

Finally, the knob turned.

The door opened a couple of inches, and I saw one terrified eye and a sheet of long blond hair.

"Daddy?"

I took a step closer, first shocked, then relieved to hear the voice of a young woman.

"Yeah, Frankie, honey. Open up the door."

Frankie studied her father, hesitated, then shook her head. "Nuh u-uh. You're too mad."

"Frankie, open the door," the man said through clenched teeth.

Again the shaking head, eye wider now.

I glanced at him, then turned to the girl. "Frankie, your daddy's not going to hurt you. He just wants to be sure you're all right," I found myself saying. "Right, Daddy?"

He turned to me, veins on his flushed neck and furrowed brow standing out. He blinked three times.

"Right," he mumbled, then looked back to her. "Right, I just need to see you, Frankie." He attempted a smile. "See that you're okay," his voice steadier now.

The girl stared at him, her one eye going to his left then right, back again, and again. I had witnessed my Stella's same suspicious gaze so many times before. Judging, searching for truth. Waiting for betrayal.

The door shut.

Silence.

Nothing.

Standing just behind him now, I could smell his fear. Sharp and musky. New sweat on top of old. His breathing sounded labored, chest rising bigger with each intake. A low growl escaped from his clamped lips. He took a step back and raised a size twelve boot level with the doorknob, poised to propel what must be 235 pounds through the door.

Click.

I grabbed his arm. His rock of a bicep twitched under the soft cloth of his sleeve. He froze and stared at me. Did he wonder, as I did, if he really wanted to know what's going on behind this door?

The door eased open and he shouldered through. I followed to find the waif-like presence of Frankie. Breasts much too big for her tiny frame, she stood like a zombie staring up at her father, on the cusp of tears.

"Where's Stella?" I heard my own voice say.

Nothing.

My voice shook. "Frankie! Where's Stella?"

Terrified eyes still locked to her daddy's grateful ones, she pointed.

Rushing past one dark doorway, I entered the main room and puzzled over what I saw. Two disheveled beds, shut drapes, TV muted, every light on, air filled with the stink of beer.

Nobody.

Confused, I doubled back to the only other room. I turned on the light. It flickered and finally caught, filling the tiny bathroom with blue light.

I knew right away something was wrong. I stared for a minute, unable to speak.

My Stella sat perched on the closed seat of the toilet. Her dirty hands clutched the dark curls covering her face.

My eyes ran down her body, taking inventory. Shirt unbuttoned lower than I ever would allow, a tiny leather skirt I had never seen. Bony knees, shiny, store-bought tan shins. Her perfect feet. Bloody feet. My horrified eyes took in her hands again. Not dirty.

I heard only the humming of the bright fluorescents, a drip in the tub, my heart pounding much too fast.

I rushed into the cramped bathroom and knelt in front of my Stella. My shaking hands clamped her thighs. Sticky. I forced myself not to pull away.

"Stella, baby. Are you hurt?"

She raised her head and I stared into her eyes. Not my daughter's eyes. Old eyes. Eyes that had seen too much.

"Tell Mama what's happened."

Frankie's daddy and I discovered the skinny body of a man much older than us lying prone, face down, between the queen-sized beds. Shards of dark glass were scattered on the floor around him. A bottle's spout stuck out from between his shoulder blades.

I bit down on my bottom lip so my screams wouldn't escape. When I turned to ask Frankie's father what we should do, all I saw was his back as he hurried to his daughter peeking around the corner. Her face full of fright, she rushed away from him and disappeared down the hall.

Hands shaking so bad, I fumbled for the phone on the bedside table. I looked down at the man on the floor by my feet and willed breath into his motionless body. But I knew he was dead, and that my Stella had a lot, if not everything, to do with the carnage laid out on the cheap green shag.

The buzzing in my ears sounded so loud I could barely make out what Frankie said to her father. "He just went nuts, Daddy. I wouldn't do what he wanted and he hit me. Stella. . . She saved my life."

In a fog, I talked to the front desk, giving them instructions, then rushed back to my Stella, now wound in a tight ball on the floor. I sat on the edge of the tub and reached out, but she tensed when I touched her. I wanted to lie down next to her, hold her, take her back to yesterday. Instead, my nails dug half-moons into my palms as I tried not to scream.

I heard Frankie's muffled sobbing, then a smack. Knowing her father had slapped her, I closed the bathroom door and waited for our worlds to unravel.

Soon, room 408 filled with chaos. Police with their endless questions, the manager screaming lawsuit, looky-loos crowding the hall, a camera's constant click and flash. My ears felt ready to burst with the noise.

But loudest of all, was my Stella's silence.

A GIFT FOR DETAILS

Alan M. Petrillo

I couldn't quite place the smell. The strong, aromatic pungency of kerosene hung over everything in the yard, but overriding that smell was the odor of something rotting. My first impression was of a dead animal, but then it hit me. Decomposed human flesh. Once you get that smell planted in the back of your brain, you should never mistake it.

"Over here. And bring that iron bar with you."

The deputies followed me to the three drums, two upright and one on its side, leaking fluid. "You two stand that drum on its end. We'll have a look inside."

As the huskier deputy pried the lid off, the stench swept over us in a wave. The younger deputy turned and heaved his lunch onto the dirt while the heavy one backed away, his eyes wide.

I shielded my nose and mouth and leaned over the rim for a better look. Staring back at me was an eyeless head floating in the kerosene, its flesh sloughed off in great gobs so that one could hardly determine it once had been human.

Shouldering the head against the side of the drum were the remnants of an armless torso, or so I guessed it to be. A foot was wedged alongside it, among other unidentifiable chunks. By the length of the sparse hair that still clung to the head, the body appeared to be that of a woman.

I stepped back and tried to draw a lungful of clear air. "Let's take a gander inside the other two. God help us if they're like this one."

One was. It contained the decomposed, dismembered body of a male. The third drum held only kerosene.

I took another look around the rear yard at 21 Drexel Road. It was littered with trash and construction debris, the rusted frame of a motor bike, and assorted lengths of wood. A six-foot adobe wall ran the width of the yard and continued along the west side to connect at the rear corner of the dwelling. On the east it terminated in a five-foot-wide battered wooden gate that spanned the distance to the building. The gate was the only exterior entry to the rear yard. A dilapidated shed leaned against the back wall, partially sheltering the three drums that now spilled their putrid fumes into the late autumn air.

Hammering on the rear door of the building next door drew no response from inside until a window on the second floor flew open and a florid face appeared.

"What's all the banging about? Can't we have a bit of peace around here . . ." The sight of our uniforms stopped her tirade.

"Perhaps you could help us, ma'am," I said, backing away from the door so I could get a better look at the woman. "Can you tell me who owns this building?"

"It's that Arthur Pratt. Always rattling around in the yard there. And usually when it's pretty dark."

"So these drums belong to Mr. Pratt, then?"

"I expect so, as he's the only one who's ever tinkering around back there. Him and that other idiot."

"And which idiot might that be?"

"Edwin. The little man with the bad leg. I only know him as Edwin, but a sorrier specimen of a man you won't find."

"Have you seen any activity in the yard lately?"

"Just the usual rustling around."

"Do you know where Mr. Pratt might be now?"

"Sure. At work. Along past the rodeo grounds at the McCreary Freight Service depot."

"Thanks for your help, ma'am. And your name would be. . . ?"

The woman took a deep breath and pushed dirty strands of hair back from the side of her face. "Miss Edna Richardson. And if you like, you can send that young deputy up here to question me more." The woman threw a lewd wink at the deputy, who quickly turned away.

"I don't think that will be necessary, Miss Richardson, but thanks for the offer."

It was getting late in the afternoon, and rather than chase across the dusty town to the shipping depot and maybe miss Pratt in passing, I decided to wait him out at his house. Two hours later, a sturdily-built man in stained workman's coveralls sauntered down the street and turned in toward the rear gate.

"Arthur Pratt?"

"Who wants to know?"

"Under-sheriff Tom Langmore." I held out my badge and identification. "Let's step into the rear yard for a moment where we can talk."

Pratt backed up a half step and checked over his shoulder as if looking for a getaway route, but thought better of it when I clapped my hand on his shoulder and pulled him toward the gate. The rear yard was now a beehive of activity as khaki-jacketed deputies and white-uniformed morgue attendants pulled dripping body parts from the barrels. Each set of parts was wrapped in newspaper and placed in a box, later to be examined by Dr. Bosworth, the county coroner. All the men in the yard had some type of cloth wound around their mouths and noses to ward off the smell, though I knew from experience that it would do little good.

"What can you tell me about those drums, and especially their contents, Mr. Pratt?"

The man's face was ashen and his mouth pursed involuntarily as if it had either secrets or contents to spill. The contents came first. When he had composed himself and straightened up, he blurted, "What the hell is going on here? What's happened to my fuel?"

"Your fuel, Mr. Pratt?"

"Yes, my drums of kerosene. I planned to bring them to the ranch that I lease near Ruby. I was planning on bringing it over there next weekend."

"And you don't know anything about the contents of the drums?"

"Contents!" he cried. "They're full of kerosene. The only thing I put in those drums was kerosene."

Either the man was a practiced liar or he actually didn't know what was in the drums. In any event, this case would take some digging into Pratt's past.

We had found the major parts of two bodies hidden in his kerosene drums, and as Pratt had no good explanation of why dismembered corpses should be hidden there, I had no choice but to hold him for further questioning. The *Daily Territorial* newspaper quickly latched onto the story of the county's first double homicide of 1910, and before I knew it, the sheriff had visited me at my battered desk and left the distinct impression that he expected a speedy conclusion to the case. After all, we had the killer, didn't we? His question had sounded more like a statement.

After performing the autopsies, Dr. Bosworth reported the bodies had been in the drums for several weeks, and perhaps months, but he had difficulty in making a closer estimate of the date because of the limited preservative effect of the kerosene and the Arizona Territory's dry climate.

I had two worthwhile leads to pursue—Pratt and the idiot, Edwin, although my wager was on Pratt. Through a lengthy interview at the sheriff's office, I learned that while he did lease a ranch near Ruby, Pratt also had a wife who no longer lived with him at the Drexel Road house. Pratt didn't want to discuss his wife until I explained that having a missing wife and dead bodies in his rear yard didn't look too good for him.

"But I tell you, I had nothing to do with those bodies."

"Then tell me where your wife is now."

The man opened his mouth as if to answer, then clamped his lips shut, closing his eyes at the same time. "I don't know."

"Your wife turns up missing and you don't do anything about it?"

No answer.

"All right then, let's try something else. What can you tell me about Edwin?"

"Edwin? You mean the simpleton who uses my shed? There's nothing much to tell. He works on bikes and motorcycles back there. Has a knack for it, some say."

"Does Edwin live with you?"

"Hell, no. I wouldn't have him. The man is filthy all of the time, drunk some of the time, and downright peculiar mostly. He lives two streets west of me on Granada Road."

"And his family name?"

"Leeson. Edwin Leeson."

"Now let's get back to your missing wife. This looks bad for you. Your wife is missing. A dead woman's body is found stuffed in a drum in your yard, along with another body. Hardly good news for you."

Pratt took a deep breath and lowered his chin to his chest as if he were taking a nap. When he looked up, a flash of resignation was on his face. "She's run off with another man."

Well, this was interesting. It certainly established a motive for Pratt to kill the woman. "When did this happen?"

"Early summer. I don't like talking about this."

"I reckon you don't. Where has she run off to?"

Pratt shifted uncomfortably in his seat, then looked me straight in the eye. "The damn woman's off to Yuma with an Irishman called O'Doul. The man was a butcher's assistant at Garratt's Meats on Campbell Road, damn him."

How do you know these details?"

"She left me a letter and wrote down the whole mess in it. It's back at my place if you want to see it."

"Yes, I'll have a deputy take you there so you can fetch it for us. And you have not seen your wife or Mr. O'Doul since early summer?"

The man hung his head and shook it slowly. "Not a hair."

Edwin Leeson lived in a single room in the rear of a ramshackle adobe house in the center of the block on Granada Road, a narrow, dirt track framed by two rows of dilapidated structures. The man did indeed have a bum leg, so much so that his left side stood an entire two inches shorter than his right. The general effect when talking to him was that the room was slanting to the side. His unnatural stance was only the beginning of his misfortunes. The man was exceptionally thin, a condition that was accentuated by his tall, stringy frame. An oversized head sat atop his thin neck and a bulbous nose projected from his face. Nature had not been kind to Edwin. And his intellect apparently mirrored his physical characteristics, being dim at best and near imbecilic at worst.

"Mr. Leeson . . . Edwin, you use the rear yard at Arthur Pratt's house to work on motorcycles and bikes?"

"Just the shed."

"And when was the last time you were there?"

"Saturday."

"When was the last time you saw Mrs. Pratt?"

Edwin put his forefinger to his temple as if he could push a button there and spit out an answer. But he made no reply and only shrugged.

"Do you know anything about the three drums in the yard?"

He bobbed his head up and down. "They're Arthur's. He has kerosene there for the ranch." Edwin snapped a grin in my direction, exposing two gaps and four blackened teeth.

"Have you ever seen Arthur putting anything in the drums other than kerosene?"

The imbecile's head swung side to side in wide arcs, his eyes bright.

I looked at the deputy and cocked my head. "Let's get out of here. This won't get us anywhere."

The proprietor of Garratt's Meats was a stout plug of a man with thick sideburns that threatened to meet in the center of his face and transform into a full beard. Michael Garratt seemingly could tell a cop from a block away and stiffened visibly as I entered his small shop.

"Relax Mr. Garratt. We're only here to question you about a former employee. That is, unless you have something else you'd like to tell us."

"I don't have anything to say to you." The man's eyes were pinched tight and his mouth formed a hard line.

"You had a man named O'Doul working for you earlier this year."

"That thieving bastard? I ran him off months ago when I caught him stealing hams. The bastard was taking them from me and selling them on the street at night for half the price."

"When exactly did you run him off?"

Garratt stroked the thick hair at the side of his face. "Must have been late in May or early June." His eyes narrowed even more. "The first week in June, I'd say."

"Do you know where O'Doul went?"

"Nope. I can't say that I care neither. He can rot in hell."

* * *

Edna Richardson's voice boomed through the thin wood of the hallway door. "Who's there? What do you want?"

"It's the police, Miss Richardson. We have more questions for you."

The door creaked open a crack and a bloodshot eyeball regarded us through the dim light of the narrow hallway. "Well, sheriff, thank you for bringing the handsome young deputy back," she said as she flung the door open. "Come in, come in."

The sitting room off the hallway was filled with shabby furniture, all heaped with stacks of clothing in states of disrepair. Miss Richardson saw me eyeing the collection.

"I take in sewing work to make ends meet. As you can see, I don't have all my good looks anymore, although I could teach this young deputy a thing or two." She winked in his direction.

"Miss Richardson, we were hoping you could tell us something of Mr. Pratt's home life. His relationship with his wife, for example."

"That wicked woman? It wouldn't surprise me that he did her in, not at all. Why the woman was catting around on him the whole time he was working at the freight depot."

"Catting around, Miss Richardson?"

"Do I have to paint a picture for you? The woman had lovers downstairs in the apartment while her husband was at work. The Irishman was the most recent."

"Would you know his name?"

"She once told me he was an insurance salesman named O'Doul. I thought that might be a lie, but I knew it wasn't insurance he was selling her."

"Was Mr. Pratt aware of this . . . relationship?"

"He must have been because a few months ago he and Mrs. Pratt had a fierce argument. You could hear it all over the house . . . likely down the block too. You could hear dishes breaking and plenty of shouting. The woman left shortly after that, or at least that's what Pratt said."

"He said that, eh?"

"Yup. He said his wife left with a friend to tend a sick relative in Yuma. But I knew the truth."

"Which was what?"

"For a policeman, you are thick-headed. That she ran off with the Irish lover, O'Doul. He came to the apartment the day after the argument. I saw him walk up the stairs and heard him bang on the door. There was some talk that I could hear but not quite make out. I got busy with sewing and forgot about them, so I never did see them leave. But you can ask the idiot, Edwin. He was in the yard working in that shed the whole day. He may have seen them leave. God knows the imbeciles of the world have a gift for the small details."

The letter from Pratt's wife was written in a spidery hand that threatened to cause permanent watering of my eyes if I read it long enough. Mercifully, it was brief.

> *Arthur: This last argument proved our marriage was a mistake. I have been seeing Patrick O'Doul for some time now and we plan to go to Yuma to live together. I'll be gone by the weekend and have no doubt you will be better off on your own. Doris*

Arthur Pratt sat with his arms crossed over his chest, his face set like stone. He had identified the scalloped silver ring the coroner had removed from the female corpse's hand. It was his wife's.

"Mr. Pratt, if you won't tell us what you argued with your wife about, we'll have to assume the worst."

"The argument had nothing to do with her death. We fought about a lot of things. She had a way of bringing out the worst in a man. A few words here and there and the next thing you knew we would be screaming at each other."

"And on the night in question?"

Pratt drew in a deep breath and exhaled noisily. "The damn woman was spending a lot of time being friendly with Edwin. I told her not to waste her time on the fool, but she wouldn't listen."

I waited for a few moments and then encouraged him to continue.

Pratt snapped his head in my direction and narrowed his eyes. "It's not what you're thinking. She wasted time talking to him about the happenings in town, things the imbecile would never be able to understand. She treated him as if he was . . . normal."

"Tell us about O'Doul."

Pratt's face remained impassive, but he swallowed hard before answering. "I know only what I've read in my wife's letter."

I glanced at the deputy, who had rolled his eyes toward the ceiling.

"Did you miss any work during June? Specifically, in early June?"

"Not a day the whole month."

The picture was getting clearer now. Deputy Williams sat across the desk from me, listening as I talked about what might have taken place. Pratt finds out about his wife's infidelity and confronts her that night after returning from work. She denies the relationship and a violent argument ensues. Pratt, whether intentionally or not, kills his wife. The next day, the lover, O'Doul, shows up for his rendezvous with Mrs. Pratt and Pratt kills him too. Pratt then dismembers the corpses and hides them in the drums of kerosene, planning to dispose of them at his ranch. It was a fine theory and had the necessary elements of motive and opportunity. The difficulty was that I still had no proof of any of it, other than two dismembered bodies. Williams suggested that another conversation with Edwin Leeson might fill in some of the blanks.

We located Edwin in Pratt's rear yard, dismantling the engine of a 100cc motorcycle. He gave us a gap-toothed grin as we approached the shed.

"Edwin, we think you may be able to help us catch a murderer. Would you like to help us?"

He bobbed his head in agreement.

"Did you ever see any men visiting Mrs. Pratt at her home when Mr. Pratt wasn't there?"

A dark look crossed his face and he nodded.

"Was a man named O'Doul one of them?"

Edwin tightened his grip on the wrench in his hand, and again nodded. "He was a bad man."

"Why was he bad, Edwin?"

"Because he was going to take her away. She told me so."

I glanced at Deputy Williams, who moved to Edwin's right. "Tell me about Mr. O'Doul."

"He came to the house and was going to take her with him. He was the reason she was going to leave, so I punished him." Edwin's eyes were fixed on some point out in the yard, his voice coming in fits and starts.

"How did you punish him?"

"I hit him with the wrench. He came into the apartment and found her on the floor. She wasn't breathing and there was all that blood in her hair. Then he saw me standing in back of the door and I hit him. I kept hitting him until he stopped breathing too."

"Did you kill Mrs. Pratt, Edwin?"

"No." The shout was loud enough to be heard a block away. "I loved her. She was nice to me. She was the only one who was nice. But she wasn't breathing . . ." He hung his head and sobbed, his shoulders shaking.

Williams reached down, and loosening Edwin's grip on the wrench, slipped it from his hand.

I gave Edwin a few moments. "Why wasn't Mrs. Pratt breathing, Edwin?"

"She stopped."

I put my most patient smile on my face. "Why did she stop?"

Edwin looked up at me and shrugged, extending his arms and turning his palms up. Slowly, he raised his hands to his face, speaking as if we were not there.

"I only wanted her to stop laughing at me. She laughed when I said she could stay with me instead of going with O'Doul. And then she kept trying to get through the door. She was going to leave with him, so I stopped her from going. When she screamed, I held her tighter and tighter and tighter, until she was quiet." Edwin's hands began to tremble as he began to sob again.

"It's all right, Edwin. I only have one more question. How did the bodies get into the drums?"

Edwin wiped his sleeve across his nose. "There was trouble for me because of hitting O'Doul. I dragged him to the shed and tried to put him in a barrel, but he wouldn't fit." He looked at me with glassy eyes. "I had to make him fit in there."

I nodded, and took a deep breath. "And Mrs. Pratt."

A flicker of panic crossed his eyes, and then he hung his head. "Yes, her too."

"Edwin, Deputy Williams is going to take you along to the station now." I nodded and Williams fitted the cuffs over Edwin's wrists, locking the mechanism tight.

Miss Richardson had been right. Edwin had a gift for small details.

EYE STRAIN

Sybil Yeaman and Rachelle Yeaman

Carla glanced at her watch as she finished reviewing her last financial report. It was six forty-five and the halls of the eye clinic had gone silent an hour earlier. "As usual, I'm the last one out of here," she muttered to herself. She liked her new role as Operations Manager but not the long hours. Her stomach growled; she'd lost five pounds since taking the promotion. She wondered if she had the makings of the next fad diet book, *The Work Your Buns Off Program.* One look at her thin frame and the masses would be sold. Carla chuckled as she gathered her purse and briefcase, then locked her desk and file cabinets. She consoled herself with the thought that it was Wednesday evening, and she was more than half way through the week.

As she flipped off the lights, she thought she heard someone crying, but it was faint, nearly covered by the sound of her heels on the carpet. Standing very still in the office doorway, she listened but heard nothing more. Perhaps the cleaning staff had a radio on down in Accounts Receivable.

With a slight shrug, she left her office. She'd hardly closed her door when she heard someone gasp and cry out.

"Help me!"

At the far end of the hall, a woman in maroon scrubs fell against the wall and slipped to her knees, cradling her abdomen. Carla dropped her purse and briefcase and rushed down the hall to the woman's side. Kneeling down, she recognized Lana Tredmore, Dr. Maron's Surgical Assistant, and put her hand on her shoulder. "Lana! What's wrong?"

"Help me," Lana whispered as she slumped over.

As Lana fell against her, Carla saw the blood, bright red and glistening—surely it was too much to be real? "Oh, my God! Oh, my God!" Carla screamed.

Lana moved her lips to say something, then lay motionless. Carla's head swam. She'd seen this in a hundred movies, the camera pulling away toward the ceiling as the dramatic music flared. But tonight, in reality, everything except Carla's heart remained still, silent—the white walls, the white ceiling, the blue and gray carpet drinking in Lana's blood.

With shaking hands, she fumbled with her cell phone. Carla took a deep breath, then dialed 911. Her voice was trembling but steady when she told the Emergency Operator to send an ambulance. As she finished repeating the address, she heard someone running down the hall. John Greel, a Financial Analyst, rounded the corner. Carla nearly shouted with relief at seeing another person.

"What happened?" John demanded.

"I don't know, but she's bleeding badly," Carla answered. "I have 911 on the line right now."

"I'm going to see if any doctors are still in the clinic," John said, and sprinted away.

Looking down at Lana, Carla tried to think of something she could do. Other than CPR, she had no medical training. Desperate, she tried to get a look at Lana's wound. Maybe she could put pressure on it to slow the flow of blood like the ER medics did on TV. But when she started to move Lana, the

Surgical Assistant cried out in pain. Carla didn't try again. She waited, breathing the scents of blood and old carpet shampoo until she started to wonder if John would ever come back or if she hadn't just imagined him. Finally, she heard footsteps.

"No one's over there," John reported.

Carla heard sirens in the distance. "I don't want to leave her, John. Can you flag down the ambulance and lead them here?"

"Sure," John said, looking almost happy to get away.

"Everything's going to be fine," Carla assured Lana, gently rubbing her arm. "The medics are coming right now. They'll have you in the hospital in a few minutes."

In a moment, the quiet hallway was a rush of medics, equipment, and a policewoman, all led by the Financial Analyst.

Relieved to have the medics take over, Carla backed away to give them room and stood next to John.

"I'm Officer Grady," said the policewoman, a short, heavy woman with a sun-worn face.

John introduced himself. Carla realized belatedly she was meant to do the same. "Carla Hersch, the Operations Manager of the clinic."

Grady nodded. "What happened here?

"I don't know. I found her like this when I left my office." Carla nodded down the hall at her door, where her briefcase and purse still lay.

"I don't know either. I came running when I heard screaming," John said.

"She's been stabbed," one of the medics reported. "The weapon is protruding from her lower left thoracic cavity."

"Stabbed?" Carla cried. She hadn't seen a knife.

Grady stiffened slightly, her eyes narrowing as she examined Carla and John with greater scrutiny. "Did you see anyone else?"

"No," they answered together.

"The assailant could still be in the clinic." Grady pulled her radio off her belt with one hand and unsnapped the leather guard on her gun with the other.

"It's possible." Carla felt a shiver of fear run through her.

"I doubt it," John scoffed. "There are exits in each hallway."

Grady called for backup.

By the time two more policemen arrived, the medics were rolling Lana down the hall on a stretcher.

"Will she be all right?" Carla asked the medics as they hurried by, but none answered.

"Stay with this officer," Grady ordered, moving down the hall with the other policeman.

Carla waited with John for a few minutes before Grady returned, her gun holstered.

"Follow me." Grady led them to the next corridor where the rest of the administration offices were and into the Medical Director's office. "Can you identify this man?"

Carla looked and gasped. Andrew Maron, the Medical Director, lay sprawled across his office floor, staring up at the ceiling. His normally crisp, white shirt and lab coat were soaked red, glossy in the epicenter like his wide, blank eyes. Carla turned away, trying to ignore the splatters of blood on his desk, peppering his paperwork and family photos.

"It's Dr. Maron," John said. "He's our Medical Director."

"I'll need to get a statement from both of you."

Carla didn't argue and followed Grady and John. Everything felt muted and slow, like walking through a heavy snow. She thought of the hysterical women in TV murder mysteries and decided the scriptwriters had it all wrong. She didn't feel much of anything, just…blank.

She got home after ten. Seven messages flashed on her phone, but she couldn't bring herself to listen to them. John had said he'd tell the Practice Administrator everything, so she didn't feel she needed to talk to anyone. All she wanted to do was take a shower. Shedding her blood-stained suit, Carla folded it and laid it in a corner on the tile floor. She let the hot water beat down on her and turn her skin red as the last few hours began to settle in on her. She began to cry as if a faucet had been turned on inside her. Great, heaving sobs rent the steaming air, followed by lesser weeping until only a whimper was left by the time the hot water started to run out. With a sigh, Carla finished showering, got into a nightgown, and went to bed. Even though she couldn't sleep, she felt better.

By six in the morning, the phone started ringing. Carla didn't answer, but listened to the messages as she made and drank a cup of strong coffee. The Practice Administrator, Steve Burnam, was the first to call and tell her the office and clinic would be closed today but open again tomorrow. In a procession, each of the six owner physicians called wanting details. She only answered when Judy Treata, the Clinical Director and her longtime friend, started to leave a message. She picked up.

"Hi, Judy. I'm here."

"Are you all right?"

Carla shrugged, ambling toward the end table to pick up her coffee. "I think so, but I'm still pretty shaken up."

"I'm not surprised. John Greel told me everything, so I won't ask any questions."

"I appreciate that. It's still too hard to talk about it." Carla gulped the last of the coffee, not minding the way it burned on the way down.

"I've got some good news that should make you feel better," Judy said.

Carla held her breath, hoping it was about Lana.

"Lana is in fair, but stable condition."

Carla closed her eyes a moment in gratitude. "That's wonderful."

"Well, I thought you would want to know. Lana's mother called with the good news."

"I can't thank you enough, Judy. It's such a relief."

Carla could almost hear Judy's nod. "Will you be coming to work tomorrow?"

"I don't know." The thought of going anywhere near that corridor turned her stomach.

"Well, don't worry about it. The place will run without you for a day. Saturday is the funeral for Dr. Maron."

"Oh, where is it being held?" Carla asked, not wanting to attend, but knowing it would be expected.

"I can't remember the name of the place, but a practice-wide e-mail went out with the details."

"Okay. I'll pull up the e-mail here at home."

They said their good-byes and hung up.

The good news and the pot of coffee revived Carla enough to get dressed. As she brushed her hair, glaring at three gray hairs she found amongst the brown at her temples, there was a knock at the front door.

"Who is it?" she asked without opening it.

"Juan Perez, Phoenix Police."

Carla opened the door a few inches and peered out, meeting the eyes of an average-sized man in his mid-thirties with black hair and a square jaw. Either that police uniform worked miracles, or he had an on-going friendship with a weight bench.

"I'm Detective Juan Perez from the Homicide Department," the policeman said, showing his ID and badge. "I need to get a statement from you."

"I gave a statement to the police already."

"I can get your statement now or we can do it down at the station," Perez said with a shrug.

Carla was tempted to tell him she'd prefer the station, but she didn't even know where the police station was.

"Let's do it now," she said and opened the door wide enough for the officer to come in. As she closed it behind him, two TV news vans and a car pulled up in front of her home.

"I'm sorry to make you go over the events of yesterday again, but it's necessary for the murder investigation," Perez said.

"I understand," Carla answered and sat with the officer in the living room. As she gave her statement, the doorbell rang, and there were several knocks at the front and back doors. "I'm not answering. It's the TV news," she explained.

"I saw them pull up behind me," Perez said as he flipped through his notebook. "Is it true you often argued with Dr. Maron?"

Caught off guard, Carla just blinked.

"Is it true you were often at odds with Dr. Maron?" Perez repeated.

"N-not often. We s-sometimes disagreed," Carla stammered, not liking the question or its implication that she had something against Dr. Maron. "Are you implying I'm a suspect?"

"Why do you think you're a suspect?"

"Because you're questioning my relationship with Dr. Maron."

Perez shrugged. "What did you argue about? Finances?"

Carla bit her lip and controlled her temper. "No. John Greel, our Financial Analyst, handles the finances. I handle staff issues, quality assurance, and grievances. Dr. Maron was demanding and often difficult to work with. He went through staff quickly, creating a high level of stress on his medical team and tension throughout the clinic."

"Anything else?"

Carla hesitated, feeling like a tattletale.

"Everything you say will be held in strictest confidence," Perez assured.

"He had an affair with his surgical nurse that ended badly." She refrained from adding that she was hardly the first.

"What was her name?"

"Diana Porte."

"You say it ended badly?"

Carla nodded. "Her boyfriend showed up drunk at the clinic's annual picnic last month and made a scene."

"Did he threaten Dr. Maron?"

"Yes."

Perez made a note. "Anything else?"

"No."

"How about medical issues?"

Carla frowned, feeling the detective was prompting her. He must have already heard something from another source. "We have a lawsuit from a poor surgical outcome."

"Can you explain the poor surgical outcome?"

"The patient was blind in one eye after a corneal transplant last week. We arranged for another specialist to repeat the procedure and repair the cornea, and some of the patient's vision has been restored. Even though the patient signed a waiver that she understood the risks of the surgery, she's suing Dr. Maron, our clinic, and our surgical center. The patient's husband threatened Dr. Maron during the post-op visit."

"It seems a lot of people were angry with Dr. Maron," Perez said, his pen still moving.

"It seems that way."

"Were *you* angry with Dr. Maron?"

"No, just concerned."

"Anything else?"

"*No!*"

"Oh, one last thing," Perez said as he rose from his chair. "I'll need the clothes you were wearing yesterday at the clinic."

Carla went to the bathroom where her suit still lay folded on the floor. She picked it up, trying not to touch the blood stains, and brought it to the living room where Perez had her drop it into a plastic bag that he immediately sealed and tagged.

"Well, thank you for your time. If you think of anything else, please give me a call," Perez said, handing her his card.

As Carla opened the front door to let the detective out, several reporters plied her with questions about the murder. "No comment," Carla said, closing the door. She massaged her aching forehead with both hands as she grabbed the phone and dialed John Greel.

"Hi. This is John," the Financial Analyst answered.

Carla didn't exchange pleasantries. "Where did the homicide detective get information that I had argued with Dr. Maron?"

"Not from me."

"You're a bad liar," Carla stated.

"I'm sorry, Carla. I might have mentioned it. The detective acted like I was a suspect. I felt obligated to tell him everything I knew."

"Well, he did the same thing to me, but I didn't implicate you."

"I told him about the affair with the RN. Do you think her boyfriend did it?" John asked. "He has a criminal record, you know."

"No, I didn't know that."

"Someone told me he did time for robbery."

Carla rubbed her forehead. "That certainly puts him at the top of my list."

"Me too. I told him about the recent lawsuit, too."

"I could tell he knew about it, because he prompted me." She lowered herself onto the couch. "Did you tell him anything else?"

"There wasn't anything else to tell, was there?"

"You forgot to tell him how you and Dr. Maron had some nasty arguments over his monthly reimbursements and expenses," Carla said.

"Did you tell the detective that?"

"No. I didn't, but next time I may feel obligated to tell him everything I know," Carla said, and hung up the phone.

Only a second later, it rang. Instead of answering, she pulled the phone cord out of the wall. She needed some quiet, and decided to take Friday off as well. She had accrued plenty of vacation, and this seemed like a good time to use it.

On Saturday morning, Carla dressed in a black pantsuit and drove to the funeral. She had never liked Dr. Maron, but felt obliged to attend and show her support as part of the administrative team. She arrived at the small stone chapel just before the service started. As she entered, she could see the casket up front surrounded by flowers. When she saw the picture of Dr. Maron on a stand next to the casket, she shivered, remembering the last time she'd seen him, bloody, and staring vacantly at the ceiling. The chapel was crowded, and Carla looked for her friend, Judy, hoping she had saved her a seat. When she spotted Judy up front, she waved, but Judy turned away.

Carla found a seat near the back. There were a lot of people she knew from the clinic sitting around her, but no one spoke to her. She couldn't miss the whispers and quick accusing glances in her direction.

As the service started, the whispers stopped, but not the glances. They couldn't really think she was the murderer, could they? "Unbelievable," she muttered to herself and rubbed her forehead, feeling the start of another tension headache. As the service droned on, one person after another got up and made tearful speeches that Carla thought were rather insincere, considering Dr. Maron's *difficult* nature. By the time the service ended, she was the first one out of the door and into the parking lot.

"Carla!" John called.

Carla turned around and stopped. Every muscle tensed as the Financial Analyst caught up with her.

"Listen, I know you're angry with me. I let the pressure get to me; I got scared." John shook his head. "All right, it's not an excuse. For what it's worth, I'm sorry."

Carla's first thought was to tell him it wasn't worth much at all, but an apology was an apology. And he *was* talking to her, which seemed more than anyone else had done. She nodded.

"And I wanted to give you a heads up; the police consider you a suspect."

"From the way everyone is acting, the police aren't the only ones," Carla retorted. "This is crazy!"

"I know," John said awkwardly.

"Why does everyone think I had something to do with Dr. Maron's death?"

The Financial analyst stepped closer and looked around in a conspiratorial manner. "Steve told me. The police searched the clinic; there were no intruders. The security system showed no one entered or exited for an hour before the murder, and we were the only ones there."

"Couldn't someone have hidden in the clinic or in one of the offices until after hours?"

"That's exactly what Steve told the detective," John assured.

"What about Diana's boyfriend?"

"He has an airtight alibi. It turns out it was his company's night at the basketball game. He was there with at least twenty of his coworkers as witnesses."

Desperate, Carla tried to think it through. "Why me? You had arguments with Dr. Maron on a regular basis."

"I was on the phone with my wife; the phone record shows it. That, and I had no blood on me."

Carla's mouth dropped open in disbelief, then snapped shut with anger. "I got blood on me while I was trying to help Lana!"

"I know," John said, taking a step back. "I was there; I saw your face. But I just thought I should tell you."

Carla composed herself and slipped into business mode. "Thank you, John. I appreciate it."

"You're welcome. Listen, this'll all blow over. They'll catch the real killer."

Carla nodded, but didn't say anything.

With the phone unplugged, the rest of Saturday was uneventful, but Carla found it hard to relax. She just couldn't get the bloody image of Dr. Maron out of her head, and was frustrated knowing everyone thought she was his murderer.

On Sunday afternoon, Carla drove over to the hospital to visit Lana, hoping Lana could remember something that would help clear her of suspicion. At the hospital, Carla didn't stop for a Visitor's Pass. Armed with Lana's room number from the office e-mail about where to send get well wishes, Carla rode the elevator up to the third floor. She located Lana's room only to find a police officer positioned outside. Carla just strolled past Lana's room and didn't stop to ask questions. It was obvious the police felt Lana might still be in danger.

When she got home, Carla tried watching TV, but nothing caught her interest. It was almost a relief to hear knocking at her door. She only hoped it wasn't the news media.

Juan Perez smiled as Carla opened the door. "I saw your car, and I was hoping you'd answer."

"I just made some coffee. Want a cup?" Carla asked.

"No, thanks."

"Wouldn't it have been easier just to call instead of driving over here?" Carla asked, leading him into the kitchen.

"Yes. Except you weren't answering the phone."

Carla blushed, remembering how she had pulled the phone plug out of the wall. "Sorry. I forgot I unplugged it."

"I didn't mind driving over," Perez assured, as he flipped open his notebook. "I have a few more questions."

"I'm sure you do," Carla said, unable to keep the bitterness she felt from creeping into her voice. She poured some cream into her coffee and took a sip. "It seems everyone thinks I murdered Dr. Maron."

"Why do you say that?"

"No one at the funeral would even look at me or talk to me. I think that's a pretty good indicator, don't you?"

Perez didn't answer but looked sympathetic.

Carla knew he needed to remain noncommittal and forced herself to do the same.

"What time were you leaving the office last Wednesday?"

"About six forty-five."

"And you saw no one and heard nothing."

She shrugged. "I was tired. It was late. I was leaving my office when I thought I heard someone crying."

"Crying?" He looked at his notebook. "You didn't say that before."

"I didn't? Well, probably because I didn't hear anything even though I stopped to listen."

"Then what happened?"

"As I closed my office door, someone called out for help and fell against the wall at the far end of the hallway. I dropped my purse and briefcase and ran down the hall to see what was wrong. When I got to Lana, she fell against me. That's when I saw the blood and called 911."

"John Greel indicated he heard screaming. Did you hear screaming?"

"I think he heard me," Carla said, a little embarrassed. "I screamed when I saw all the blood. It took me a moment to get over the initial shock before I could call 911. My hands were shaking so badly that I could hardly dial the numbers."

"Your quick action may have saved her life."

"Thank you for saying so. Have you gotten a statement from Lana?"

"Yes."

"What did she say?"

"She walked into Dr. Maron's office. He had already been stabbed and then she was attacked."

"Is that all?" Carla pressed.

"That's all I'm able to disclose," Perez said. "However, I have other information I'm able to discuss with you. We think Dr. Maron and Lana were both attacked with the same weapon, a letter opener."

Carla raised an eyebrow. "Dr. Maron had a letter opener that looked like a medieval sword. He kept it on his desk."

"Did you ever use the letter opener?"

"No!" Carla exclaimed.

"Can you remember anything else about the incident?"

"No," Carla said, and stood up to signal the end of the conversation. She had had enough of leading questions and implications. "If you need to ask me any more questions, I will come down to the station."

"Thank you again for your time," Perez said as he stood up and closed his notebook. "Please be sure to call me if you can think of anything else."

Carla couldn't escort the detective out the front door fast enough and shut it behind him. Leaning against the door after locking it, she wondered how this had gotten out of control. What she needed was a good lawyer. Judy Treata's brother was a lawyer, but she wasn't about to call her. Not after the way Judy had turned her back at the funeral. That had hurt more than anything else.

Thumbing through the phone book, Carla picked out a couple of the largest law firms in Phoenix. If Juan Perez had any more questions, she'd make sure she had legal advice before answering. She fell asleep with the list of attorneys clutched in her hand.

Carla woke up before her alarm rang, refreshed and ready to go to work. She was done being the victim of everyone's suspicions. She put on one of her best suits and decided she looked good. She headed for work, surprised by how her resolve had empowered her. At the clinic, she greeted everyone cordially and went to her office. To her surprise, the day went quietly. Since everyone avoided her, no one interrupted her work. By the time she answered all her e-mails, responded to her voice mails, and opened her paper mail, it was late afternoon and time to go home. "No more late nights for me," she promised herself as she locked her desk and file cabinets. She would go home the same time as everyone else. What didn't get done would have to wait until tomorrow. As she picked up her purse and briefcase, the Practice Administrator stepped into her office.

"Do you have a minute?" Steve Burnam asked.

Carla didn't have a chance to answer. The Administrator sat down in one of the chairs across from her desk. She resigned herself to sit down and hear what he had to say. By his demeanor, she could tell it was serious and probably not good news.

Steve Burnam cleared his throat and began. "The owners think the clinic has gotten top heavy with upper management. They've decided to eliminate two positions, Operations Manager and Financial Analyst."

Carla didn't say anything. She was so surprised by the declaration that she was at a loss for words.

"I know you've worked with us for many years, and I want to reward you," the Administrator assured. "The practice is compensating you with a month's salary for each year you worked here. Combined with your vacation time, you have a whole year's compensation."

Carla looked down at her hands as she clenched them until the knuckles were white. She had worked hard for the clinic for ten years and now it was over just as if it were nothing.

"This should give you plenty of time to find another position," Steve added as he passed Carla a plain while envelope with her name on it.

As Carla accepted the envelope, Detective Perez knocked on her office door. She couldn't believe things could get any worse, but here he was to arrest her. She was sure of it.

"Am I interrupting anything?" Perez asked.

"No, we're finished here," Steve Burnam said as he started to get up.

"Please stay for a moment," Perez urged. "We've had a break in Dr. Maron's murder."

"All right," Steve said, sitting back down.

"We have a confession."

"Really? Who did it?" Steve asked, stealing a glance at Carla.

"Lana Tredmore."

Carla was stunned. "H-how could that be?" she stammered, relieved by the news, but confused at the same time.

"But she was stabbed," Steve said, as much a question as a statement.

"She got emotionally involved with Dr. Maron," Perez started to explain.

"How could that be? She was only here a few weeks," the Administrator scoffed.

Perez shrugged. "Nevertheless, they were having an affair. She was coming down the hall to see him, expecting to go out for dinner. She overheard him making airline reservations for two to Las Vegas. Only he wasn't making them to go with her. He was going with Diana Porte."

"Crime of passion," Carla said.

"Yes. She used the letter opener from his desk."

"But she was stabbed," Steve repeated.

"To cover the attack, she stabbed herself. When we traced Dr. Maron's last call to the airline, the airline representative indicated she thought she might have heard an altercation on the phone but was cut off. Since they record the calls for security and quality assurance, we were able to get a copy of the conversation. It was Lana's voice in the background."

"Are you sure?" Steve asked.

Perez nodded. "Yes. When I confronted her with the facts this afternoon, she made a full confession. She went berserk with jealousy. She didn't mean to kill him and was deeply sorry. I thought you should be the first to know."

"Thank you so much," Carla said, as she got up to shake his hand. "You don't know what this means to me."

"Oh, I think I do," Perez said with a smile as he left.

Carla grabbed her purse, her briefcase, and her favorite picture off her desk, and headed for the door.

"Um, do you have a moment, Carla?" Steve asked.

"No, I'm finished here," Carla said, and left.

At the exit, Perez was waiting. When he saw Carla, he opened the door for her.

"Thank you," Carla said. "And I want to thank you again for personally coming over to clear my name."

"I had an ulterior motive for coming," Perez said. "Now that you're not a suspect, I'd like to ask you out. Are you free for dinner tonight?"

Carla touched the compensation envelope in her pocket and smiled. "As a matter of fact, I happen to be very free."

THE LIBRARY MURDERS

C Rose

For some reason, the library is different today. Perhaps it's something in the air or the new paint that dots the outside building. Dorey walks inside unaware that Mrs. Treesdale has already started her routine of dusting, cleaning and complaining about the library's volunteers—her, in particular.

Mrs. Treesdale heads the Library in Partners with Community and also sits on its Board of Directors. In the process of modernizing the library, she makes all their lives miserable.

Harriet, Dorey's boss each Wednesday, waves her over. "Mrs. Pain-in-the-Book has arrived early today. Watch yourself," Harriet warns as she strokes some loose bleached blond hairs out of her eyes.

"You're just on time." Harriet points to a stack of magazines that are piled on top of each other. Dorey understands from Harriet's gesture that she wants them put in chronological order.

"And please, pick that one up." Harriet nudges her head toward a newspaper on the floor. Across the bold black print splashes, "Library Serial Killer Sought. Cyanide Poisoning the Cause of Two Deaths."

Dorey's medium frame slouches over the paper. Thick brown hair bunches up into a sloppy bun. "Oh, did you read this?" slips out of her thin-lipped mouth. But her question remains unanswered.

Harriet abruptly returns to her office. Dorey assumes Harriet's behavior has to do with the early appearance of Mrs. Treesdale.

Dorey's a volunteer and works at this library once a week. Three other days of the week, she's at different county libraries. All the volunteers have an opportunity to travel to the many branches.

Besides stacking and sorting books, Dorey categorizes them into genres. She thinks her job is important. It gives her plenty of time to use her imagination and create jingles that swirl in her head and spill out onto paper, when available. Mostly, they erupt out loud.

"What a way
to spend the day.
I've got the knack,
to stack—
and stack...
and stack."

Dorey peers out to see if anyone hears today's rhyme and wanders over to the mystery section. No one's in view, but a distinct clean scent disperses above her head. While intrigued with the aroma, perhaps a man's after-shave, she notices a tan hand crunched between two Agatha Christies.

It has to be Roger, another volunteer. Her hand grabs for his, thinking she'll force his hand forward playfully. But instead of Roger's hand being held in the sweet spot of hers, Dorey pulls too hard and ceramic fingers fall at her feet. Next to the broken pieces lie the two Christie books, both with pages open.

Laughter roars from the other side of the bookcase. Dorey peers through an open area of the shelf only to see Roger laughing hysterically. Tears drip down his face while he struggles to catch his breath.

"Damn you, Roger."

But he's too busy blowing his nose to hear her. He carefully folds his handkerchief, places it in his pants pocket and crimps the folds in the front of his pants. He lingers in a graceful pose after putting himself back in order. Dorey spies on him and fantasizes, imagines herself with Roger. But her thoughts return to reality and the many times she's caught him and Debra, a salaried employee, fondling between the bookcases, holding hands and rubbing their bodies against each other.

One time last week, Roger threatened Dorey, "If I ever catch you sneaking up on us again, you'll be sorry." He knows how Dorey feels about him and teases her every chance he can get. He warns that he will intentionally misfile books, knowing Mrs. Treesdale will blame her, not him or Debra. "After all," he reminds her, "Mrs. T and I are tight. We speak the same language." Then he says under his breath, "Some day she's going to push somebody too far and . . .," he claps his hand, "bingo. Poor old woman ends up dead."

Dorey's job requires patience, care, and endurance; a knowledge of the alphabet, and of course, a love and respect for all the authors that spend their lives writing their stories.

"Murder, murder
let's not utter,
touch the dust
but not the cover.
A little bit here
a little bit there,
books have lives
by authors who care."

Harriet overhears and glares through her glass office at Dorey.

Dorey continues to do her work, systematically alphabetizing the C's in the mystery section. She methodically returns the Agatha Christie books to their shelf and cleans up the shattered clay clumps.

This modern library possesses more novels and magazines than any of the others in the county. The shelves move back and forth to provide enough space for this inventory and legroom for the library users. A button, four feet above the floor, is housed at every fifth bookcase and regulates the motorized platforms to open and close.

"Walls that move
from front to back
hold the books
and keep them stacked..."

Mrs. Treesdale suddenly appears before Dorey can finish her poem. "Can't you do anything right?" her chicken-like head squawks. "You and Roger, both of you, come here. I want to show you what you should be doing." They follow her, like obedient children, to the non-fiction section. Dorey and Roger gather around as Mrs. Treesdale wipes away dust from the spines of nearby books.

"We must abide by the library rules and be sure to re-stack our books correctly." She points to Dorey. "Someone has not been filing properly." The evidence, a misfiled Sherlock Holmes, *The Hound of the Baskervilles*, rests in Mrs. Treesdale's hand and has obviously been placed in the non-fiction section. She ends her sermon and waddles off. Roger leaves to find Debra, who usually hides in the backroom doing as little as possible.

Standing by her cart, between non-fiction and romance, Dorey doesn't pay attention to a creak that whips across the ceiling. Walls shake and vibrate as they slowly glide inward. Bookcases seem to swell as their squeaks resonate louder and fuller. A vacuum appears to seal off air. Dorey is frozen and confused. She can't move as sweat forms on the surface of her skin. She rubs at the small balls of water that dot her arms and legs. She thinks she is yelling, "Can anyone hear me?" The roaring shelves muffle her small voice. She finally pounds her hands against the books as they move closer and closer. Hopeful that noise—any noise—will get someone's attention, she drops books, taking them from their ledges and slams them onto the floor. *Who could have been so careless?* Her heart beats violently; she feels as if it will drop out of her chest.

"Okay, everyone, don't panic," Harriet calls from her office. "We seem to be having some problem with a mechanized shelf." She rushes to disable the electronic unit, bumping into Debra on the way to the controls.

Everything stops. There's a moment of silence and Dorey hears something fall.

Harriet hurries over, her face flushed. "Are you okay?"

Dorey nods, then touches the shelves that should have stopped moving since she was standing in the aisle.

"I know. I know. Everything should have worked." Harriet apologizes. She dashes off to reprogram all the sections.

The fallen books have to be picked up. There are quite a number of them that are opened and piled on top of each other, their dog-eared pages in all sorts of disarray. Cautiously sorting the books back into a Dewey Decimal system, Dorey's eyes scan the last shelf. A streak of sunlight captures something bright on the other side of the bookcase. Upon closer examination, she realizes it's the glow from a ring around a wrinkled finger. Nearby is an opened book. Dorey concludes it's Roger fooling around again, and makes her way to the mystery section to confront him. Instead, she discovers Mrs. Treesdale, lying soundless on her stomach, and spread-eagled across the floor. Her blood drips along one side of her body. The Sherlock Holmes mystery she held earlier is on the floor by her right leg. Carefully, Dorey picks it up by its inside pages.

"Help," bellows Dorey's voice, one that she's not familiar with.

Harriet runs over, finds her between the sections and wraps her arm across Dorey's shoulder. Luckily, no library visitors have as yet entered the building.

Harriet bends down and feels the limp body for a pulse. "I can't feel anything." She cups her hand over her mouth, and covers a little smirk in her upper lip, along with a secret between her and Mrs. Treesdale.

She yells for Roger, "Call an ambulance. Right away!"

Debra runs past everyone, hurries over and takes charge. She has had CPR training and with her little body is somehow strong enough to turn Mrs. Treesdale over. She sees bubbles around Mrs. Treesdale mouth, applies pressure to her lungs, then her heart and tries mouth-to-mouth resuscitation. She feels for a pulse and lifts Mrs. Treesdale's eyelids. Debra tilts her head, and answers all the questioning faces.

"She's dead."

Debra wipes her hands along her tight fitting spandex skirt. "I did what I could," she says, and disappears.

Harriet calls out to Roger again, "Phone the police, too." She turns to Dorey. "What happened? Did she get crushed in the shelves?"

Instead of answering, Dorey recites:

> "Boil and toil
> troubles that bubble.
> Crazy lady that did the jig
> falls on her head
> and ends up dead."

Harriet eyes Dorey, as if she's fed-up with her poetry. A moment later, Harriet motions to the floor. "Look."

Bloodstains tie-dyed onto the beige tile lead to a note by Mrs. Treesdale's hand, now tinged in a bluish hue. Harriet swipes up the note with her perfectly manicured nails and murmurs, "Look at the H and then the B. You will find your killer." An odd expression shrouds her face. "Okay, what the hell is this supposed to mean?" She carelessly puts down the note on the shelf closest to her arm.

"It means—murder," Roger declares, standing behind Dorey, who can feel his warm breath trickle down her neck.

Debra comes out of hiding and huddles near Roger.

"Murder?" Harriet broadcasts. "What'll we do now? We're being audited by the County Supervisors. They want to use this site as the exemplar for others in the District." Harriet extends her neck toward the dead body lying in a pool of blood by the mystery section. Her nails rap on the shelf.

Dorey looks at Mrs. Treesdale, so quiet and still. She notices a pink color across Mrs. Treesdale's lifeless face. The Sir Arthur Conan Doyle remains tucked in Dorey's covered arm.

Everyone remains stationary until the EMTs, Medical Examiner and police arrive. The thick-necked EMTs do everything they can to revive the body. When the Medical Examiner officially pronounces Mrs. Treesdale dead, the Police Officer in charge demands a thorough investigation. But his inexperienced detective tosses aside a crumpled note found on a bookshelf near the body.

Dorey knows what will happen next.

After the police questioning, she will retrieve the pair of gloves that are hidden in a special drawer in the backroom. She will become enamored by their familiar bitter almond scent and will quickly find a new place to hide them. She will hand the Sherlock Holmes book, *The Hound of the Baskervilles*, to Debra, and ask her to re-stack it since Dorey will be at another library the next day.

After fulfilling Dorey's request, Debra will never again tamper with the library's moveable bookcases.

HIS LITTLE DARLING

Maralee Reiner

"Dave Parry's dead!" Annie Jenkins shouted, running into the backyard. She thought she'd find her husband Will up on a ladder trimming the elm, but instead she found him over by his toolshed.

"Hon, I told you I'd fix your ironing board just as soon as I finish the trees." At eighty-three, Will Jenkins was slightly deaf and hadn't heard her. One glance at his wife, though, told him she wasn't talking about household chores. "What's the matter?" he asked as he lay the clippers back on a shelf and closed the door of the tool shed.

It took Annie a second or two to catch her breath before she could explain. "Didn't you hear? They found Dave Parry lying dead on the sidewalk over by the desert lot!"

"Now just take it easy, Hon." Will reached out to steady her. Annie Jenkins had a serious problem with her lungs and shouldn't have been running. The doctor had made that very clear on their last visit. "Hon, this is a senior citizen community. Dave was an old man," he said gently. He put his arm around her and led her back toward the house.

Coyote Trail was indeed a senior citizen community. Almost everyone who lived there was in their seventies and eighties. Will and Annie had been together for almost sixty years, ever since they'd met at a shooting contest back in Oklahoma. Annie won, much to Will's chagrin. But once he took a good look at her, he decided she was the girl for him, and he had pursued her like mad till she finally succumbed to his charms.

Through all the years, they'd been a team sharing all kinds of adventures, the good along with the bad. In his working days, Will had been an ironworker and the two of them traveled throughout the southwest with their two little girls in tow as he helped build bridges and dams. Even after he retired, they kept on traveling for awhile in their big, fancy motor home. But when Will had a massive heart attack down near Tucson, they knew it was time to settle down, preferably near a hospital. That's how they'd found Coyote Trail. There were two big hospitals nearby.

"They don't think Dave's death was natural!" Annie remarked.

"Why's that?" Will slid open the patio door and led her into the kitchen.

"There was blood on him."

"Who told you that?"

Annie looked at her husband defiantly. She just knew he wouldn't believe it. "I talked to Joanne," she asserted, as if she'd talked to God. Then she pulled out a chair and sat down at the table.

"Joanne," Will repeated, scratching the side of his face. He sat down, too. Joanne McMerton was secretary of the homeowners' association, and practically ran the place even though there was a property manager. She was always the first one there whenever there was a problem, and in Coyote Trail, there were quite a few problems.

The development consisted of small houses called 'vacation villas' by the realtors. They were little houses, or casitas, designed for outdoor living. They had been built with "snowbirds" in mind. Those were the people who could afford to maintain two homes and liked to come to Arizona for the winter. But not everybody in Coyote Trail was a snowbird. There were some others, like the Jenkinses, who lived in the casitas year-round.

Unfortunately, a number of these year-round residents were odd, cantankerous, and just plain miserable people. As a result, it was like a war zone when they held the quarterly homeowners' meetings. The litany of complaints never seemed to end. At one of the meetings, Dorothy Avery came to say she'd complained to Arizona Fish and Game because the landscape crew cut down a tree with a bird's nest in it. Max Stein reported that he'd helped Pete Dominic hang up a sunshade, but he said Pete didn't have a permit. Sally Myers angrily reported her neighbor had painted his mailbox brown instead of the customary black. Dave Parry's name came up a lot. That was because he offended everyone sooner or later.

"Joanne said she was just about to call Milt Kreiler," Annie asserted. Milt was the property manager of Coyote Trail, the fifth one in seven years. And he was having second thoughts about handling Coyote Trail because of all the problems.

"Was it Joanne who found Dave?"

"No, Angus Galbraith. He was just about to take his dog Maizie over to the lot when they turned onto Commodore Drive and he saw Dave lying there."

"Maybe a coyote got him," Will suggested. "You sure he's dead?"

"Of course." Annie gave Will a dirty look. "Joanne said he was stabbed."

They were both quiet for a minute. "No one much liked Dave," Will commented.

"I know," Annie replied. "But you can't just go around killin' a guy because he's an old fool." They were both quiet again. "I wonder who could have done this?" she said quietly.

Then, all of a sudden, she exclaimed, "It wasn't Allyson, if that's what you're thinking."

Allyson Kendall was their next-door neighbor. Younger than the other residents, Allyson was a widow and still worked. She'd moved into Coyote Trail with four pets and then befriended a stray cat. That had sent Dave Parry over the edge. He decided to try to sue her. The only problem was Allyson wasn't violating any of the CC&Rs, so he ended up with egg on his face and a hefty legal bill.

Will and Annie had come to Allyson's defense after the incident and the three of them were now good friends. Allyson looked out for the old couple and they, in turn, helped out with her pets when she was at work.

"You're right." Will nodded and said, "More like old Dave would go after Allyson. She kinda put him in his place." She had told everyone what Dave had done. Then she had gotten herself elected vice president of the community. Now he was more or less a pariah in Coyote Trail.

They heard a tiny sound over in the corner. It was Bebe, their eight pound Chihuahua, making little noises as she slept. "She looks like an angel," Annie commented. Before they'd gotten Bebe, Will and Annie lived kind of a dreary life. Their daughters lived in other states and rarely visited. They had only each other and their doctor appointments. Bebe had brought a lot of sunshine into their lives.

The little dog lacked for nothing. She had toys and games and beds all over the little casita—and when that wasn't enough, she had the run of all the bottom cupboards in the house. Will built an enclosed walkway all the way from the back patio to her own little play area under his precious trees. She even had a plot of grass! No coyote was going to come over the wall and make a quick meal of his little darling.

Annie pampered Bebe, too. She sat with her on her lap when she was reading or sewing, and she carried her from room to room when she was doing her housework. When the Jenkins weren't fussing over Bebe at home, they took her driving with them in a special basket. When she wasn't resting in her little basket, Will carried her around in a fluffy pink blanket.

"She's dreamin'," Will said, gazing adoringly at Bebe.

"Hmmm." Annie nodded, smiling proudly at her little baby. She had the coloring of a pinto pony and there was a diamond-shaped spot right on the top of her head. When she was awake she had perky little eyes and gave the appearance of a demure little angel, but truth be told, she could come on like a vicious attack dog if she felt threatened.

"Maybe it was one of the gardeners," Annie suggested. "Dave never liked them coming on his property. 'Member he had a shouting match with Alberto when he trimmed his tree?"

"Alberto's long gone. We've had Carlos for several months now," Will reminded her.

"Didn't Dave nearly punch Charley Davis when he couldn't see well enough to pick up his dog's poop?" Annie asked, looking up at her husband. Charley was nearly blind.

"If old Charley couldn't see the 'poop' at nighttime, I don't expect he could see Dave either," Will remarked. "Anyways, I heard his wife put him in Glenview last week because his memory is gone."

"How'd you know Dave died at nighttime?"

"Isn't that when he takes his walk? You know, he was scared to death to show his face after that fiasco with Allyson."

"I suppose the police will soon be coming around and talking to us all." She got up and went to make a pot of coffee.

Will shoved his chair back and stood up suddenly. "Now why would they be doing that?"

"Oh, sit back down. Don't get your feathers all in a stir. They're not going to interrupt your tree cuttin' time," Annie scolded.

Will was not a man who could sit still long. They had bought the biggest lot in Coyote Trail just so he'd have a garden to work in. He loved trees and had planted a lot of them. That morning he'd told Annie he was planning to trim the big elm, and at his age, it would take him most of the morning.

"Joanne told me we're not supposed to go anywhere. They're coming around to each of our houses. It'll take them awhile to get over here."

"We can't leave?" Will asked.

"We're not supposed to," she answered. "But we weren't going anywhere, anyway.

"I'm hungry," Annie said. She had baked a cinnamon coffee cake when they got up at 5:00. After that, they went to the gym where Will did the cardiovascular exercises his doctor recommended and Annie walked the indoor track. But now it was close to 7:30. "Let's eat." She went over and took the cake out of the pan, put it on a glass dish, and carried it to the table. Then she came back with the coffee pot and poured them each a cup.

"Why did Angus call Joanne and not the cops?" Will asked.

"Maybe he was hoping she would just go over there and bury him. That would have been the end of our problems with that cantankerous old fool." Annie laughed.

Some people at Coyote Trail referred to Joanne McMerton as "the general" because of her take charge attitude. Will Jenkins might be the president of the homeowners' association, but everyone knew Joanne was really in charge.

Will cut himself a giant piece of cinnamon coffee cake. "No it wouldn't," he joked back. "There's still Dorothy Avery. She's almost as crazy as Dave Parry." He'd gone over to Dorothy's house once when she had plumbing problems, but as soon as he walked in the door, she had warned him not to get fresh with her. "That woman is bonkers!" he declared.

A little bell jingled and they looked over to see that Bebe was awake. She stretched and shook her tiny body and headed for the table. "She smells the cake," Will said, beaming. "Good morning, Merry Sunshine." He reached down and picked up the diminutive dog. Bebe was really Annie's dog, but she tolerated Will, especially when he had food in front of him.

"Don't give her anything," Annie warned sternly. "You know the vet said absolutely no people food."

"I'm not feeding her," Will said, getting defensive. "I'm just picking her up." He gave Bebe a kiss on her button nose. "When do you think the cops will be coming?"

"I don't know. More coffee?" Annie got up to get the pot. "I imagine they're still over with Doris."

"Yeah, the wife's always the first suspect." Will laughed.

"Will Jenkins!" Annie said, pulling back the pot. "Or the husband. If they found me dead, you'd be their first suspect."

"You're real cute when you get mad, Honey Bunch," Will teased. "She's cute, too," he said, nodding at Bebe.

When they'd finished eating, Annie started gathering up the dishes and silverware. "Well, go on, get out of here and go back to your trees," she said. "I'll come and get you when the cops get here."

Will handed over Bebe. "It's your turn for the little darling," he said, but he didn't get up. Instead, he asked, "Why do they want to come here?"

"That's how they do it on television," Annie replied. "They talk to all the neighbors. Then they look for suspects." She caressed Bebe's ears, and gently placed her back in her basket.

"What do they want to talk to the neighbors about?"

"To find out if they've seen anything," Annie said. "Like maybe when you took Bebe out last night you ran into Dave."

"I did no such thing!" he protested.

"I was only suggesting," Annie said. "You get up on the wrong side of the bed or something? One minute you're joking and the next you're snapping my head off." She went into the laundry room and brought back her folding. "By the way, was it better to walk her at night?"

"Nah, I don't think it was such a good idea. It's too dark for her. We can go back to the mornings, as long as it's early. We don't want her to burn her little paws."

Annie noticed that he still didn't seem to be in that much of a hurry to go back to trimming his trees. She guessed he was just as interested as she was in Dave's mysterious death.

"Someone around here killed him, you know."

Will didn't reply.

"Dave never went anywhere else," she said, explaining why it had to be a local. They were both silent again, and then she added, "I guess they'll have to check everyone's knives and garden tools."

The phone rang and Annie went over and picked it up. "You heard right," she declared. "Stabbed right in the belly!" Annie didn't know that for sure, but she guessed that's where old Dave had got it. She went on talking for a few more seconds and then hung up.

"That was Beverly." She was their neighbor on the other side. "She says there's a roadblock now."

"How'd she hear?" It never ceased to amaze Will how fast gossip traveled in their little colony.

"Heard it from Mavis Turley," Annie said. "You know, the Turleys live right next to the desert lot. I wonder if they saw or heard anything last night. But, come to think of it, so do the Stanleys. That's where Allyson went last night, you know. They were watching movies," she added.

Will didn't catch most of what she said. "Nah, the Turleys go to bed at seven o'clock," he said. "Matt told me he likes to get up at four."

"That doesn't mean anything," Annie snapped. "You don't know when Dave was killed. They mighta heard something."

"Dave was out later."

Annie looked up. "And how do you know that?"

"It's still hot at seven o'clock. Dave wouldn't go out till it cooled off."

Bebe squirmed in her basket. "If you don't want her, I'll take her outside with me," Will offered. He bent down, picked up Bebe, and started for the sliding doors.

"No, don't take her, Will," Annie cried out. She hurried over and planted herself between Will and the slider. "You'll get busy cutting those trees and forget all about her. It's way too hot for her to be outside. It's supposed to reach 107 today."

"Forget the baby?" He ruffled Bebe's ears affectionately and handed her back to Annie. The little dog wiggled herself around in Annie's arms as if she understood every word they were saying and was enjoying all the fuss being made over her.

Will smiled sweetly at his wife as she put Bebe back in her basket. "I wouldn't let anything happen to that dog, *not one little thing.* You know that." He went over and slid open the door. "Now you two girls have a nice day, and I'll be back later."

Will went outside, but he didn't go over to the elm tree. Instead, he went back to his workshop. It was next to the wall that separated his house from Allyson's. He reached in, pulled out a pair of clippers, and began wiping them again while he thought of what to do. He must have wiped them fifty times already that morning. All he could think about was the night before. Annie had called him in when dinner was ready and instead of putting away the clippers, he'd slipped them into his pocket. Then after dinner there was the baseball game and then the news. By the time that Bebe needed to go out, he'd forgotten all about the clippers in his pocket.

He'd gone out alone with Bebe because Annie wasn't feeling well. They usually just went down Turquoise Lane, made a left on Commander Drive, then went back up Shotgun Way which eventually became Turquoise again. It was a circle. He should have stuck to that, but he'd decided to take Bebe over to the lot. They'd never gone there before.

They were on their way back when suddenly the clippers had sprung open inside his pocket and jabbed him in the leg. He let go of the leash to grab them. At just that moment, Dave Parry came toward them. Now, Bebe didn't like strangers any time, but especially not when they came upon her unexpectedly. She usually yapped a lot before she'd attack, but not this time. Dave saw her coming and yelled, "Will Jenkins, you get that damned rat beast away from me!" Will saw him lift his leg and knew what was about to happen.

"No!" he'd yelled and charged at Dave. That's what he'd meant to do, anyway, but he had the clippers in his hand. After the two collided, Dave staggered, clutched at his chest, and slid to the ground.

Will reached down to check on Dave, but he was already dead. "Oh, ma god!" he groaned. He'd never done a crooked thing in his whole life. But now he realized he was a murderer. He'd go to jail. Annie would be all alone, and they'd probably put her in a home. They'd take Bebe away for sure.

For a couple of seconds Will had just stood numb, waiting for the neighbors to come out and find him with the body, but nothing had happened. Incredibly no one came! Finally, when he couldn't stand it any longer, he snatched up the clippers and Bebe and rushed for home.

The sound of a woman's voice startled him.

She looked as surprised to see him as he was to see her. "Good morning," Allyson Kendall said. Her ladder was right up next to the wall, and it looked like she was climbing over. "I was just trimming my tree."

"Is that what you were doing?" Will replied. He thought it odd that she was cutting her trees in her work clothes. She was a physical therapist at a big hospital in town and had on a white uniform.

"I sure could use those clippers," Allyson said. "I got all the way up here and didn't think to bring both the big clippers and the little ones."

"Oh, you don't want these clippers," Will responded, drawing back. "There's something wrong with them." He started to put them back inside the tool shed.

"Oh, yes, I do. I want *just* those clippers," Allyson answered. They made eye contact, and Will reluctantly handed them to her.

"How's Bebe today?" she inquired as she snipped off a tiny piece of a branch.

"Fine, just fine."

Allyson turned back to look at him. "That's good," she said and then added very gently, "Bebe wouldn't have survived if he'd kicked her, you know."

"What do you mean?" But even as he asked, it hit him like a bolt of lightening. Allyson knew what he had done. It was horrible. It was terrible. If only he'd put away the clippers. If only he had just stuck to his usual route. If only Annie had come with him. If only Dave hadn't come along.

"What are you going to do?" he asked.

"You can't possibly leave those clippers in your tool shed," she declared, ignoring his question. "They may not look in there today, but eventually they will. They have scientific tests that can find blood even when it's invisible to the naked eye. And you can't drive out of here and throw them away right now without causing suspicion." She added, "But *I* can. I'm the only one around here who still has a job."

Will tried to track what Allyson was saying, but his mind was racing.

"You listening to me?" Allyson Kendall's voice interrupted his thoughts. He hadn't the slightest idea what she was talking about, but, at least, it seemed she wasn't going to turn him in. "I think my plan will work, but we have to be sure we've covered our bases."

Will nodded and then asked, "How did you? I mean how come you know?"

"I was coming out of the Stanleys' house and was crossing the street when Dave met up with you and Bebe. It all happened so quickly, and then you ran away. I thought at first you had shoved Dave hard enough to knock him out. But that seemed pretty incredible. You're tall, but Dave Parry was built like a rock.

"When I bent down to look at him I saw blood, and I couldn't find a heart beat. I noticed that the wound was up on Dave's shoulder. I've watched enough crime shows to know what that meant. They'd be looking for someone tall. Will, you're the only man at Coyote Trail tall enough to have made a wound like that. You'd be their number one suspect!

"I just couldn't let that happen. After all, it was an accident. You hadn't done it intentionally. You were just trying to save Bebe. Annie depends on you. And Bebe, what would happen to Bebe if you went to jail? It would serve no purpose. Then an idea came to me. I took Dave's wallet."

"What did you do that for?"

"To make them think it was a robbery."

"Ain't nobody around here that would rob one of us," Will protested, thinking of all his elderly neighbors.

"But we're not the only ones around. They've been building that apartment complex back there in the empty lot. A construction crew has been working there for weeks."

"They won't know I did it?"

"Not likely, but they may make you show them your tools, so you'd better let me keep those clippers. Okay?"

"They're going to look at all my tools?" he asked helplessly.

"Maybe not today, but one of these days," she answered. "It's just what they have to do. Oh yeah, and I wouldn't mention to Annie about taking a different route last night."

Allyson reached over and patted Will on the shoulder. "Just leave it to me. I'll take care of it. I'll stash the clippers and the wallet as far away from here as I can, in two different places."

Allyson climbed down off the ladder and disappeared into her house.

As soon as she got inside, Allyson dialed Annie to give her last minute instructions about her pets.

When Allyson finished talking, Annie asked excitedly, "Did you hear about Dave Parry?"

"Yeah, I heard about it," Allyson answered. "By the way, sorry I couldn't go with you to the rec department this morning. We watched movies over at the Stanleys' till ten. It was all I could do to get up this morning."

"You were right where it all happened!" Annie exclaimed.

"What do you mean?" Allyson asked.

"Dave was found right next to where you were watching movies."

"You don't say."

"Angus found him right by the Stanleys' and Turleys'."

"Is that right?" Allyson commented. "I walked home and didn't see a thing."

"Is this your early day?" Annie asked, changing the subject.

"Yup, I should be home by six. Got plans?"

"You can come and see our videos of Bebe at the vet's office. I'll make Sangria."

"Sounds swell. You two take care." Allyson hung up. Then she went out and got into her car. She drove down Turquoise Lane and turned right on Commander. The roadblock was set up right at the entrance to the community.

"Do you live here?" the officer asked.

"Yes," Allyson replied with a pleasant smile.

"Didn't you hear that we've asked all the residents to remain in their houses for the next few hours?"

"Oh, I can't do that," Allyson protested. "I work at the hospital and I've got to get there."

"I thought this was a retirement community," the officer said.

"It is, but I'm not quite retirement age yet; I have to work." Didn't Joanne McMerton explain about me?"

"You don't happen to live by the desert lot where they're building those apartments," he asked.

"No, but I was over there at the Stanleys' watching movies last night, and they do," she admitted.

"Did you hear or see anything unusual?"

"No, but we were watching movies till late."

"Really? What time did you leave?"

Oh, I guess it was about 10:30 or a bit later. I walked home," she offered.

"Did you see anyone else out walking?"

"Not a soul," she lied. "During the summer months there's only a few of us living here. Most of these places belong to snowbirds."

He nodded. "Yeah, we understand there aren't many of you here," he replied. "What about people who might have driven by?"

"I did see a black van going down Commodore, now that I think of it!"

"You did?" he asked eagerly. He pulled out a little booklet. "I gotta get some information from you before I let you go."

Allyson couldn't believe her ears. It was even easier than she thought it would be. "Why is that?"

"We think the old guy was killed by someone who was trying to rob him," the officer explained.

"A stranger?"

"Sure. We'll talk to the residents, but it's more likely it was some guy from the construction crew. But those contractors sometimes use day laborers and don't even keep records. We might never find the killer."

"That's what you think?" Allyson asked, trying as hard as she could to contain her joy and immense relief. They were going to get away with it! The authorities thought it was a robbery, and now, with her information about a black van cruising the area, she'd given them even more fuel for the fire.

"You older folks better be careful. Lock your doors and don't go out alone at nighttime. It's not safe."

"Thank you, officer, I'll take to heart your very good advice," Allyson answered and pulled away. She waved to several other officers. "Have a good day," she called out politely. There was no doubt about it. Allyson Kendall was certainly going to have a good day, and so would Will and Annie Jenkins and their dog Bebe.

MURDER IN MIND

Audrey Thibodeau

Wrapping my hands around the warm coffee mug I leaned back in my rickety chair. It had been a bad night, too much booze and bad poker hands. I knew trying to bluff old Barney on that last hand was a bad idea. "Oh, well, that's the way it goes," I mused aloud. The piercing ring of the phone broke my train of thought.

My girl Friday, Bright Eyes, stuck her head in the door and said, "There's a woman on the phone." She popped her gum and added, "Says she has to talk to you, now!"

My chair clunked to the floor and I grunted, "Who is it, and what does she want?"

"How should I know?" She turned, swung her hips and walked into the outer office with her carrot-colored pony tail swishing down her back.

Yeah, Brenda was a real pip. I inherited her from my friend Carlos when I took over this dying detective agency. Some days, like today, I wondered what I was doing here. My grandfather had been a cop in Boston. After he died, my parents moved to Arizona where my father was a cop. He got himself killed when I was too young to remember, so I thought I had to enter the police academy. My old lady had been right when she said it was a rotten idea. She didn't need to lose a son, as well as a husband. One year on the street had taught me that gig wasn't for me. Instead I wound up here.

"Yes, this is Clarence Maloney," I said crisply into the phone. Love that name—it speaks of respectability and honesty, right?

"You must help me," a high, nervous, but cultured voice answered.

"Yes ma'am, how can I help you? First, what is your name?" I asked, sounding very business like.

"Oh, I am sorry. My name is Elaina Soundstrand," and she spelled it for me. "Please help me, my husband is going to kill me."

Her quick intake of breath and a choking sob numbed my ear. I jotted the name on a pad. She certainly had my attention. "Please, calm down madam. Where did you get my name?" I asked in a dead calm voice, thinking I could get her to answer that question and quiet her panic.

"Yes." She sounded calmer but there was still a definite note of panic in her voice. "Oh, yes, I found your name in the Yellow Pages. Please, I desperately need your help.

I sipped some coffee before replying. After all, she was the one in need of help. No reason to rush.

"Okay." I looked down at the pad. "Mrs. Soundstrand, what makes you think your husband is going to kill you?"

"Oh, I know he is planning to murder me." There was a slight gasp and then she said, "Oh, dear I cannot talk about this on the phone. Please, meet me."

"Okay lady." I was getting a little tired of this conversation and my head was pounding. "Why don't you come to my office."

"I am sorry but I couldn't possibly come to that part of town."

My patience was growing very thin. I looked up, and Brenda was in the doorway waving a newspaper. I beckoned her to come in, as I half listened to the voice on the phone trying to explain why she couldn't come to my office.

Brenda plopped the paper in front of me and pointed her carmine fingernail on an item on page three. The name she was pointing to was Henry Soundstrand.

I waved Brenda away and interrupted the voice on the phone, "Is your husband Henry Soundstrand?" My eyes were scanning the article. Well, well, it seems the old boy was in a pot of trouble, besides wanting to murder his wife.

"Yes, Henry is my husband. Do you know him?"

"No, I've never had the pleasure, but this article in the morning paper indicates he's in a bit of a dilemma, wouldn't you say?"

She didn't choose to reply to that. Instead her voice reached a high crescendo as she repeated, "Please I must meet and talk with you."

Was I interested now? You bet. I could see big bucks here. Now that my brain had kicked in, I did know the Soundstrand name, the town's richest family, no less. Maybe I could even pay my rent this month and buy a decent suit.

"You say where and when Mrs. Soundstrand," I crooned into the phone.

"There is a restaurant out on Highway 16, called Kads or something, no one would know me there."

"You mean Kadads?" I asked.

"Yes, I think so, can you meet me there at 2:00 this afternoon?"

"Sure, how will I know you?"

There was a brief silence. I could visualize her running, mentally, through her wardrobe deciding what would be appropriate for a nondescript roadhouse.

"I will be wearing a navy tailored suit with a white blouse, low-heeled navy shoes, I think, and a red carnation. Does that sound all right? I won't be over dressed for this place?"

"No, that sounds fine." I swallowed a chuckle. This dame calls me up hysterical, says her husband is trying to kill her and now she's worried about wearing the correct attire to a crummy roadhouse.

As soon as I set the phone down, Brenda bounced into the office, her red mini skirt swinging around her very pretty legs. Now that would be more appropriate for a roadhouse, I thought.

"Well," she asked, between cracking that infernal gum, "do we have a client, or what?"

I looked at her, and wondered why she had to wear all that stuff around her eyes. Actually, her baby blues might be pretty if they weren't surrounded by all that black stuff.

"Yeah, could be. How about some more coffee and some aspirin?"

Carefully, word for word, I read the article in the paper. It sounded like the guy had enough trouble without plotting to kill his wife.

As I gulped down the aspirin with the lukewarm coffee, I decided this woman was probably paranoid and I would be wasting my time, but what the hell, I could always bill her for conference time. She ought to be good for a few hundred bucks.

I went to the door and yelled at Brenda not to disturb me until 1:00. I shut the door and stretched out on the worn leather couch.

By 1:15, I was in my ancient Chevy tooling along to the edge of town. Calvin, Arizona was a medium sized town, but the midday traffic was plentiful. As I eased my way over to make a turn I wondered how a fancy woman like Mrs. Soundstrand knew about a dive like Kadads.

There were only a couple of pickups and a jalopy in the parking lot when I swung my wheels into a parking spot. Good, I was early. That would give me a chance to grab a booth by the window and size her up before she came in.

As I stopped just inside the door to look around, the bartender looked my way and then turned back to the television. Two guys in ragged jeans sat on stools at the bar, absorbed in the tube. A couple in a dim booth in back was absorbed in each other. I sauntered over to a booth where a grubby window looked out on the parking lot.

After a few minutes a tall, gangly waitress in a soiled apron appeared.

"What'll it be Bub?" she asked, swiping at the table with a not-too-clean rag.

"Give me anything in a bottle," I mumbled. I sure wasn't going to drink anything out of a glass in this joint.

Yeah, I'd been here, long ago. It was never a very classy joint, but I didn't remember it was this bad. The cracked leather seats, the filthy windows, the slovenly bartender and waitress, were disgusting. No way was I going to let Mrs. Soundstrand come in here. My, wasn't I being chivalrous? What had she thought this place was? Well, when she drives up, I'll go out and we can talk in her car. That should be private enough.

When I saw the shiny yellow Mercedes Sport pull in next to my heap, I threw a few bucks on the table and darted for the door. Before she had time to check her face in the mirror and get out of the car, I was opening the passenger door.

She turned with a startled expression and said, "What do you think you're doing?"

I stuck out my hand and said, "I'm Clarence Maloney."

She ignored my hand and pulled back toward the door. "I said I would meet you inside, not out here in the parking lot, and how do I know you are who you say you are?'

This was a real looker. Her honey blonde hair swung around her shoulders, and her eyes were a violet color that bored into me. I pulled out my P.I. license and held it toward her. Without touching it she peered closely at the picture, and then stared at me. It wasn't a very good likeness and my hair had been longer and darker, now it was streaked with gray, but it was close enough.

"Very well," she finally said, "but I prefer to go inside."

"Lady," I said. I was really getting ticked off at this dame. "Have you ever been inside this joint?"

"Certainly not," she replied stiffly.

"Then take my word for it, you wouldn't like this place."

"Very well," she murmured. "However, I will not sit here with you, in a parking lot in full view of heaven knows who. What do you propose we do?"

"Okay, Okay. I'll get in my car and you can follow me. I'll find a secluded spot where we can talk."

"I am not sure I want to follow you to some 'secluded spot', as you say. How do I know I can trust you?"

My first thought was to tell her to find someone else. She was a classy lady with her expensive car and clothes, but she was a loony toon. On the other hand if I blew this, no fee. So, I took a deep breath and in a very calm voice I said, "Mrs. Soundstrand, you called me and didn't want to meet in my office. I come all the way out here and you don't want to talk in the car or follow me some place else. What exactly do you want to do?"

"I'll drive and you follow me. Would that be acceptable to you?" She looked at me with those luminous eyes that had just a whisper of a tear. So, what could I do but agree. I've always been a sucker for a woman's tears.

She reached for her keys, and I walked to my car. She didn't waste any time backing up and swinging that beauty around toward the exit. It made me wonder if maybe she'd had second thoughts and was going to ditch me. No, when I pulled out of the exit she was driving slowly north on the highway, away from town, and obviously waiting for me to catch up. We'd gone about ten miles when she signaled a right turn.

As I followed her down a graveled road, I remembered this was the way to Strand Lake. It had been a W.P.A. project back in the Thirties. Now, ten years later, it was a beautiful mountain park. I hadn't been out here since my high school days. Guys came here to skinny dip or bring girls to park.

She made a sharp left without signaling, and I had to hit my brake to keep from rear ending her expensive machine. I maneuvered in quick behind her just in time to see her pull into a driveway going up a hill toward a cabin. What is this? Maybe I was the one who shouldn't be so trusting. My right hand felt under my coat for my piece. Now who was getting paranoid? She was a woman, and I was a hulk of a man, what was I worrying about?

I parked behind her and watched as she got out of her car. How could I help but admire long, nylon clad legs with the spike heels? She went up the steps to the cabin, turned and looked back at me.

Pocketing my keys I quickly got out of the car, and took the steps two at a time. Whatever she had in mind, I could handle it.

When I reached the porch, she was still fiddling with a ring of keys. Since the windows of the cabin were boarded over, it was obvious it hadn't been used for sometime.

"Here it is," she exclaimed, as she fitted a key in the lock.

The big oak door squealed on its hinges as she pushed it back and stepped inside.

This lady was no fragile female. I was over six feet and we were eye to eye. Sure she had on heels, but still she was no dainty doll. And, I might add, she was very well put together.

Mrs. Soundstrand surveyed the dim room, and then said, "It's dusty and hasn't been used for some time."

No kidding, I thought, as I stepped gingerly across the threshold, and stopped. It was too dark to see anything, and I began to wonder if she had someone else waiting here. Again, my hand went to my belt and the feel of cold steel reassured me.

"Do you have some matches? The electricity is off but there is an oil lamp on the table."

Wondering if she lured men up here often, for whatever reason, I quickly fished in the pocket of my jacket and handed her a folder of matches. My eyes were beginning to adjust to the dark, and I could make out shapes of couches and chairs, all draped with sheets. It was a cavernous room. I couldn't even see a wall on the other side.

"Is this your place?" I finally asked, as she fussed with the lamp. Silly question, she had a key.

Flicking a sheet off one of the couches she ignored my question. "Sit down and let's talk." It sounded more like a command than an invitation, but what the hell, that's what I was here for, to talk.

She sat, or should I say, sort of curled up with her long legs tucked under, at one end of the couch. I sat on the edge of the other end and surveyed the room again. The glow of the lamp cast shadows on the paneled walls, the draped paintings, and a pile of rolled up rugs against one wall. From the amount of dust on the floor—we had actually left footprints—and on tops of the tables, this place hadn't been used in a very long time.

I looked back at Mrs. Soundstrand and raised my eyebrows in a questioning look. Why bring me way out here to the lake and this deserted cabin when we could have talked in my office?

My mind was framing questions I hoped she could answer, when she reached across and touched my knee. "You don't remember me, do you Mal?"

My head jerked up. I looked into those gorgeous eyes and shook my head. Mal, no one called me that anymore.

"I can see you don't remember. Why should you?" She continued, when she saw my puzzled look. "I was just a skinny, bothersome kid of ten, always tagging after my brother and his friends on Clancy Street. My brother was Chuck O'Hara." She paused, looked at me, and waited to see my reaction.

My head was spinning. Clancy Street was where I grew up okay, and yeah, I remembered Chuck. We'd had some great times together with Bud and Brick and some other guys. I hadn't seen any of them in years. This gorgeous creature couldn't be Chuck's bratty sister we were always chasing away. I began to wonder what kind of a con this was.

Before I could ask her what she had really gotten me out here for, she started talking.

"My husband really is going to try to kill me. I need help. I really did look in the Yellow Pages, and when I saw your name, I knew you were someone I could trust. I'm sorry about doubting you. She paused, then looked at me and laughed. "You'll have to admit you have changed some, and certainly, I don't look much like I did at ten. Do you think it's an improvement?"

I was still staring at her and trying to remember Chuck's sister's name. It certainly wasn't Elaina. I nodded agreement, and said, "Oh yes, you have changed. You've changed so much I would never have recognized you, and I don't remember that your name was Elaina."

"Oh, that. Actually my name was Mary Elaine, and I hated it. When I went to business school, I dropped the Mary and changed the spelling to Elaina. I really am Chuck's little sister."

"Okay. Maybe I believe you, but why all this cloak and dagger stuff? Why didn't you tell me on the phone who you were and then come to my office? And why meet at that crummy dive? If you've lived around here all your life, you must know that's not a place for a pretty lady like you, even in its best days."

She smiled at me, and batted her eyelashes. "Mal, that's the nicest thing you ever said to me. Those are reasonable questions, and I haven't any answers. Does it matter? The important thing is I really do need your help. You read about my husband in the morning paper. And yes, he is in deep financial trouble. He has a ten-million-dollar insurance policy on my life, and believe me when I say his business is much more important to him than I am."

"Has he threatened you?" I was finding it a little hard to believe her.

"Not actual threats, but our marriage has been over for several years. We live in the same house, hardly ever see each other and are only polite in front of the servants. Don't you see he doesn't need me, but he does need the money from that insurance policy."

"How do you think he's going to kill you? With poison, a gun or what?"

"Oh, no."

She dug in her purse for a hanky. Oh, boy, here come the water works, I thought, but she blew her nose and looked at me with a faint smile.

"He's much too smart to do anything obvious. It will look like an accident."

"What exactly is it that you want me to do?" I asked.

"I want you to follow him, don't let him out of your sight, watch his every move. He might tamper with my car, and if you were watching him, then you would know. I have money of my own that I put away. During the first years of our marriage, he was very generous. Since I know what it's like to be poor, I wasn't about to ever let him throw me out without a dime. So, anyway, I can pay you."

"Look, Mary Elaine or Elaina, or whatever, I think you're worrying your pretty head about something that isn't going to happen. Henry Soundstrand is a businessman who has hit a snag. It doesn't mean that he won't straighten out his affairs, and it certainly doesn't mean he's going to murder his wife. I don't think spending the rest of his life in jail is an option he would want."

"Jail, don't be silly, he would never go to jail. I told you he's smart. He'll make it look like an accident, and no one will ever question him. I can see you don't believe me, so I guess I'm wasting my time." She stood up. "Shall we go?"

Suddenly, I was watching bucks walk out the door. I jumped up and spun her around. "Not so fast. I didn't say I didn't believe you think your husband is going to try to kill you, I'm just not sure what I could do to prevent it. But if following him around will ease your mind, then fine; I'll do that. First, I want some proof that you really are who you say you are."

Without saying a word, she reached in her purse and pulled out a faded photo, and handed it to me. I walked over to the lamp and peered at the dim figures. Yes, it was a picture of Chuck, Bud and me in front of my house on Clancy Street. I almost knocked her over when I turned around. "Where did you get this?"

"Don't you remember, I took it. My parents had given me a little brownie camera for my birthday."

"Yeah, I do remember, but when I asked for proof of who you were, I meant are you really Elaina Soundstrand? I guess I'm really wondering how a little girl from Clancy Street is married to a prominent, rich man?"

"I see. Shall we sit down?"

After we were seated on the couch, this time side by side, she continued, "I graduated from business school and went to work for the Soundstrand Chemical Company. Eventually I was promoted to Henry's secretary. Don't look at me like that, I know what you're thinking. Oh, well, I guess it's true. I set out to marry him, and I did. After all, isn't it every girl's dream to fall in love and marry a handsome, rich man? Like I said, in the beginning everything was fine. We were in love, but then he changed. I knew a little about the business. After all I had been his secretary. Suddenly, he stopped talking to me about the business. When I asked questions, he told me to mind my own business. But I knew things weren't going well, and he was worried. Then about a year ago, we had a really big fight and he hit me."

"What was the fight about?" I asked.

"Money, of course. He was being really tight with the money and screaming at me about my charge accounts. Anyway, that was when I moved to the guest room, after he hit me."

"So, why suddenly do you think he's going to kill you?"

"It's the way he looks at me. The night we had the fight he actually called me names. He said I was a tramp from the wrong side of the tracks, and he was sorry he married me."

"Then why don't you get a divorce?" To me that was the sensible solution.

"A divorce, are you kidding? There has never been a divorce in the Soundstrand family. He told me once there never will be. It's a matter of pride. Oh, dear," she glanced at her diamond studded watch, "I didn't realize it was getting so late. I want to get home before he does."

We stood up and she extinguished the lamp. When we walked out the door she leaned over and kissed me on the cheek. "Thanks, Mal, for listening, and for agreeing to help me."

She locked the door, turned around, thrust an envelope in my hand and ran quickly down the steps to her car. When I reached my car she was turning around and heading down the driveway.

Slowly, I crawled into my car. Sitting there for a moment, I began to wonder what in the world I was getting myself into. Finally, I opened the envelope. Inside were crisp five-hundred-dollar bills, ten of them. I'd never seen that much folding money all at once. My mind envisioned all I could do with five big ones. There was a note with her address, and she didn't want me to call her. She said she would contact me.

I put my hands on the steering wheel and stared down at the sunset over the lake. Yes, I remembered who the Soundstrands were. It was all coming back to me. The lake was called Strand. Old man Soundstrand use to come out on the porch of that cabin and yell at us kids when we got too noisy on the beach. Little Mary O'Hara had come a long way, and no one was going to harm a hair on her head if I could help it. I stuffed the envelope in my inside coat pocket and headed back to the office.

The door was locked. Good old Brenda had gone home. It was just as well. I didn't need her nosy questions. The real question was where was I going to stash this money. I couldn't carry it around with me, the banks were closed, and I sure wasn't going to leave it in this office. I flipped on the light and leaned back in my chair.

"Think this thing out Maloney," I said aloud. Then I jumped up and ran out of the office, slamming the doors. Where was my mind? Mary, I couldn't help thinking of her as Mary, gave me all that loot to protect her and here I was sitting around wondering where to hide the money when I should be out there tailing her husband.

By the time that I got to my car, checked the address and figured out the quickest way to get there, I was feeling like a jerk. The house was on Strand Hill, where else? I'd have to find out if he was home. As I cruised by the big house on the hill, I could see only one light upstairs, but the downstairs was lit up like a Roman candle.

Parking the car down the street, I wondered how I was going to find out if Soundstrand was in the house. How did she think I was going to protect her, or keep track of his movements if they were both inside? I was still wondering why she hadn't moved out. She said she had some money, and there had been no mention of kids.

While I was mulling all this over, I heard sirens coming down the street. I hit the pavement running, when two police cars and an ambulance pulled into the Soundstrand driveway. I was breathing hard when I reached the open front door. Sgt. Harris, a bulky middle-aged cop, whirled around and said, "What are you doing here, Maloney?"

Ignoring his question I asked one of my own, "What happened here? Is she dead?"

Before Harris could answer, Elaina ran into the hall and threw herself at me. I grabbed her arms and held her away from me. A thin robe clinging to her body didn't leave much for imagination. Her face was puffy and tears were streaming down her face. Obviously he hadn't killed her, since she was standing there being hysterical. I steered her over to a chair and looked at Harris. "What the hell is going on here?" I demanded.

"Her husband's dead, but I still don't know what you're doing here." Harris's voice was a flat monotone.

I explained, as best I could to the Sergeant, knowing I'd never been one of his favorite people since I quit the force. He grunted and walked further into the immense marble-floored hallway. Then he turned and said, "See if you can quiet her down so we can find out what happened."

Elaina was still sobbing hysterically. She looked up through a veil of tears when I touched her arm. "It's so awful, and I'm so scared. Please stay with me," she said in a choked voice.

"Elaina," somehow the name seemed appropriate in these surroundings. "Calm down and tell me what happened."

She brushed at her tear-stained face, pushed back her long blonde hair, took a deep breath and without looking at me she said, "He tried to kill me. I told you he would. But, I was wrong; it wouldn't have looked like an accident. I was in my room getting dressed for a dinner party. Henry barged into the room and started yelling at me. I told him to get out, and suddenly he waved a gun in my face."

She managed a choked sob as she continued, "I was stunned with shock, but somehow I rushed past him and headed for the stairs. I heard the gun go off. I turned and Henry was tumbling down the stairs. The gun was still in his hand. I screamed, but of course no one heard me because it's the servants' night off. I ran over to him, but I knew he was dead. I sat there on the floor for I don't know how long. I couldn't seem to move. Finally, I went to the phone and called the police. Oh, Mal, I'm so thankful you were near by."

"Mrs. Soundstrand, we're going to need a statement from you. But I guess it can wait until morning. Do you want a doctor or can we call someone to stay with you?"

Harris was standing at my elbow and had heard her story. He bought it, for the moment. He turned to me and asked, "Are you sticking around?"

"No, I think I've seen and heard quite enough for one night." Elaina didn't even look at me as I walked out the door.

"So long, Mary Elaine O'Hara," I mumbled to myself. "You think you've won it all, and you sure made a fool out of me." *But baby*, I mused, *you better watch out for Sgt. Harris. He may seem like a big, soft teddy bear, but he's smart.*

Patting the envelope in my pocket I walked back to my car.

ABOUT THE AUTHORS

BARBARA McARTHUR. (p 9) Barbara's inspiration for *"Smalltown Heart"* was her grandmother's hometown in Arizona—filled with fascinating characters—who always had opinions . . . about somebody else! Her debut novel, *"Requital,"* is scheduled for publication in summer, 2005. A romantic thriller set in Havana, Cuba in 1959, it promises to deliver an unforgettable love story besieged by danger, conspiracy, betrayal and a vengeful obsession. Barbara's next project, the first of the Florencia mysteries, finds murderous intent in the least likely place . . . a senior resort community—proving that you're never too old for murder! Barbara lives in Woodinville, Washington, thriving on the chaos and joys of a large family living nearby . . . and dreams of winters in Arizona.

MICHÈLE STAPLEY (p. 23) is an accomplished painter of contemporary genre paintings that focus on the gestures and body language found in small moments of human drama. Many of her short stories take place in the art world, as does *"Incident on Main Street."* Her mystery novel, *"The Death of Art,"* was published in 2004.

MARIA GRAZIA SWAN. (p. 39) Maria is a Phoenix, Arizona-based writer who immigrated to America from Italy in 1969. She has published several short stories and articles. In 1990 she received an award from the Women's National Book Association for an essay on breast implants. Her first full-length mystery, *"Love Thy Sister,"* was published by Zander Books in 2001. She presently writes a monthly singles' column for an online magazine while working on her first non-fiction book. Ms. Swan is a real estate professional who caters to single buyers. She is the divorced mother of two and the grandmother of two.

ROBIN MERRILL (p. 51) lived more than half her life in Alaska, the most interesting years as a Homesteader in the wilderness. From there, she moved to California, where she graduated from university while her two children finished high school and began college. She has lived in Arizona for the past twelve years, more content now with heat than snow. She writes romantic suspense and mystery suspense, and has completed two unpublished novels.

SUSAN BUDAVARI (p. 67) has written two psychological suspense novels and several short stories since moving to Arizona in 2000. Prior to that she worked in chemical research and in scientific information management in the pharmaceutical industry in New Jersey, and served as Editor of *"The Merck Index,"* an internationally recognized encyclopedia of chemicals, drugs, and biologicals. She is an avid photographer and painter.

SUZANNE FLAIG (p. 77) is a freelance writer and editor whose nonfiction works have appeared in numerous magazines and newsletters. She started writing mysteries in 1998 after previous careers as a piano teacher, professional roller skater, lab technician, and foreign language teacher. She lives in Phoenix, Arizona and has completed a mystery novel set in her home state of Pennsylvania.

REVA SPIRO LUXENBERG. (p. 91) If you like Sadie at seventy-four in *"The Call from Beyond,"* then you're sure to like her in her younger years when she solves the mystery of who killed her son Jeffrey's professor in Oxford in Reva's novel, *"Murder at the Second Lily Pond."* Reva took an early retirement as a social worker to concentrate on writing. Her latest novel, to be published in the fall of 2005, is *"Grand Army Plaza,"* the story of a Jewish widow who adopts a black boy. The author lives with her husband, Jack, in Sun Lakes, Arizona. Her hobbies are reading, gambling, golf, and making videos.

PATRICIA KLEMME (p. 101) was raised in the Midwest and has a B.A. in Education from Nebraska Wesleyan University. She has lived in Arizona over thirty years. She has worked as a teacher and businesswoman and is currently a home healthcare nurse. She enjoys travel and reading. Pat and her two cats live, work, and play in central Phoenix.

HOWARD "DOC" CARRON (p. 113) was born in Brooklyn, New York, is married and the father of 3 daughters. His career includes: photographer, musician, teacher, ceramist, silversmith, sculptor, painter, wood block artist, writer (editor and writer for Cigar Lovers Magazine), librarian and chef. Degrees: BS, MLS, PhD. He studied with Alfred Van Loen (sculpture), Hodaka Yoshida (wood block), Robert Von Neuman (drawing), Joseph Schoenfelt (jewelry), Nancy Chin Ma (cooking), and Charles Loloma (jewelry). Howard taught overseas from 1969 to 1993 Elementary, Secondary and College (Japan, Okinawa, Korea, Azores, Philippines and Germany). He is currently a Supervisor of Adult Reference in Gilbert, Arizona.

DEBORAH J LEDFORD (p. 123) is a suspense thriller writer with two completed novels and seven original screenplays to her credit. All of her works delve into the psychological aspects of her vivid characters. Although *"Stella"* is Deborah's first published piece, she has written a number of mainstream literary short stories which are being considered for publication at this time.

ALAN M. PETRILLO (p. 129) lives in Tucson, Arizona where he writes full-time for national and regional magazines and newspapers, as well as mystery and thriller fiction. He has been a reporter and editor for daily news organizations, including the Schenectady Union-Star, the Amsterdam Recorder, United Press International and the Associated Press. His historical mystery, *"Full Moon,"* was published in 2005 by JoNa Books. Excerpts can be viewed at www.fullmoonmystery.com. Petrillo also is the author of five books on antique firearms and one on the New York court system.

SYBIL YEAMAN (p. 141) lives in Arizona and is a Regional Director for a national surgical center corporation. Although she has written predominantly historical fiction, she is an enthusiastic follower of medical mysteries. Her daughter, **RACHELLE N. YEAMAN** is a Creative Writing and German Studies major at the University of Arizona. Her main interests lie in fantasy and science fiction. Despite devoting most of her time to her studies, she hopes to complete her first novel by graduation.

C ROSE (p. 159) is currently completing her first mystery novel, *"Evil In 'Zona"* (a dog mystery), starring Guggy, a miniature poodle, with a nose for trouble. *"Evil In 'Zona"* takes place in the western desert. Rose also writes under the name of CR Bolinski and Carole R Seldin and has published poetry and flash fiction. She lives with her husband in northern Arizona.

MARALEE REINER (p. 167) was inspired to write *"His Little Darling"* when she moved to Sun City West, Arizona from California in 2000 and learned first-hand about HOA (homeowners' associations). Maralee is a bilingual marriage-family counselor.

AUDREY THIBODEAU (p. 183) has had non-fiction articles published in magazines across the country, from Arizona, Colorado, Wisconsin to New Hampshire. Her weekly column, *"Grandmother Used To Say,"* has appeared in newspapers in Arizona, New Hampshire and Rhode Island. It was a weekly feature for seven years in New Hampshire. Audrey now lives in Mesa, Arizona and writes fiction.

ABOUT THE PUBLISHER

Red Coyote Press, LLC, founded in 2004, specializes in publishing high quality mysteries of all sub-genres.

RED COYOTE PRESS, LLC
PO Box 60582
Phoenix, AZ 85082
www.redcoyotepress.com